"Where is he?"

she heard Jake demanding furiously as he reached out to grab hold of her wrist.

"He...? What he?" Lucianna queried in bewilderment.

"What he? The one you've dressed yourself up like that for, of course," Jake told her bitingly.

Instinctively, she placed her free arm across her breasts, her eyes flashing daggers of embarrassed fury at him.

"It's a bit late for that," Jake told her scathingly. "You might as well be stark naked—you damn well nearly are."

"I am not," Lucianna denied. "I'm wearing the new underwear *you* told me to buy."

"*I* told you to buy?" Jake checked himself and frowned.

"Oh God," she heard him mutter under his breath, "I must be crazy doing this."

Doing what? she tried to ask, but found she couldn't say a single thing, for the very simple reason that Jake's mouth was now covering hers and silencing every sound she tried to make.

PENNY JORDAN has been writing for almost twenty years and has an outstanding record: over one hundred novels published, including *Power Play,* which hit the *New York Times* bestseller list, and more recently, the phenomenally successful *To Love, Honor and Betray.* With over 60 million copies of her books in print worldwide and translations in more than seventeen languages, Penny Jordan has established herself as an internationally acclaimed author. She was born in Preston, in Lancashire, England, and now lives with her husband in a beautiful fourteenth-century house in rural Cheshire.

Recent Books by Penny Jordan

Penny Jordan

MISSION: MAKE-OVER

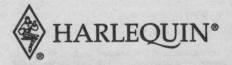

TORONTO • NEW YORK • LONDON
AMSTERDAM • PARIS • SYDNEY • HAMBURG
STOCKHOLM • ATHENS • TOKYO • MILAN • MADRID
PRAGUE • WARSAW • BUDAPEST • AUCKLAND

ISBN 0-373-12158-X

MISSION: MAKE-OVER

First North American Publication 2001.

This edition published by arrangement with Harlequin Books S.A.

® and TM are trademarks of the publisher. Trademarks indicated with ® are registered in the United States Patent and Trademark Office, the Canadian Trade Marks Office and in other countries.

Visit us at www.eHarlequin.com

Printed in U.S.A.

CHAPTER ONE

'No LUCIANNA...? Where is she—trying to breathe life into some hopeless wreck of a car?'

Janey Stewart smiled at her husband's best friend as the three of them shared the informal supper Janey had prepared.

'No, not this evening, Jake,' she informed him in response to his wry question about her sister-in-law and the youngest member of the family, the only girl. Lucianna had arrived after her mother had already produced four sons, and, as a consequence of that and, more tragically, of the fact that Susan Stewart had died after contracting a rare and particularly virulent form of viral pneumonia when Lucianna was only eighteen months old, had grown up treated by her brothers and father almost as if she were another boy.

'She's out,' she added in further explanation as he raised a questioning eyebrow. 'Saying goodbye to John.'

'Saying *goodbye*... The big romance is *over*, then, is it?'

'Not exactly. John's going to work in Canada for three months. I suspect Lucianna was rather hoping that he might suggest putting their relationship on a bit of a permanent footing before he left.'

'She hasn't a hope in hell,' said David, her husband and Lucianna's eldest brother, who now ran the farm where he and Lucianna and the rest of the Stewart brothers had been brought up and where in fact Lucianna still lived.

'She's *never* going to get herself a man whilst she goes around dressed in a pair of baggy old dungarees and—'

'It isn't all her fault, David,' Janey interrupted him gently. 'You and the others have hardly encouraged her to be feminine, have you? And you've certainly done your share of helping to frighten away potential men-friends,' she pointed out mildly.

'If you mean I've made it clear that if a man wants Lucianna to share his roof and his bed with him then it has to be with the benefit of a wedding ring, then what's wrong with that?'

'Nothing,' Janey allowed, adding dryly, 'But I seem to remember you worked pretty hard to convince *me* that we ought to move in together before we were married...'

'That was different,' David told her firmly.

'I hope this relationship with John does work out for Lucianna,' Janey continued worriedly. 'After all, she's twenty-two now, not a teenager any more.'

'No relationship is going to work for her until she stops acting like a tomboy...' David told her decisively, adding, 'Perhaps you could give her one or two hints, Janey, point her in the right direction.'

'I've tried, but...' Janey gave a small shrug. 'I think she needs someone to *show* her, *not* to tell her, someone to build up her confidence in herself as a desirable woman and not—' She broke off and smiled teasingly at her husband's best friend. 'Someone like you, Jake,' she told him.

'Jake?' David hooted with laughter. 'Jake would never look at anyone like Lucianna, not after the women *he's* had running after him. Remember that Italian model you went out with, Jake, and that New York banker, and what happened—?'

'Er…you're married to *me*, thank you very much,' Janey reminded her husband firmly. 'Perhaps you aren't the right person, Jake, but she does need help of some kind from someone, otherwise I'm very much afraid she's going to lose John and she'll take it very hard.'

'He really means that much to her?' Jake frowned, his dark eyebrows snapping together over eyes of a particularly clean and sharp blue-grey colour, all the more striking set against the warm olive of the skin tone he had inherited from his Italian grandmother and the thick dark hair that went with it.

His height and breadth of shoulder he had inherited from his paternal relatives; the great-uncle from whom he had inherited the farm and manor house whose lands bordered on the Stewarts' farm had been of a similarly impressive build.

'I rather fear so,' Janey told him quietly. 'She needs help, Jake,' she added, 'even if she herself would be the last person to admit it, especially…'

'Especially to me,' Jake concluded for her.

'Well, you do rather have the knack of making her bristle,' Janey smiled.

As the grandfather clock in the passageway struck the hour, Janey's smile turned to a small frown.

'John's flight will be leaving in half an hour and then Lucianna will be back.'

'Wanting a shoulder to cry on?' Jake asked Janey perceptively.

'Luce never cries,' David informed him. 'She's not that type.'

Really there were times when her husband could be maddeningly dense, Janey reflected as she listened to David. One of the reasons Lucianna was such a tomboy, so uncomfortable about showing her emotions, was that as a child she had been taught by her older brothers not to do so.

It was a pity that Lucianna didn't get on better with Jake because he would certainly have been the ideal person to help her to understand why her relationships with men never developed properly. And it wasn't just that, as an extraordinarily charismatic and sensual man, he had the experience, the know-how, the awareness to help her, he also rather unexpectedly and, in Janey's view, very charmingly for such an intensely male man, had a very compassionate and caring side to his nature as well, even though she knew that Lucianna would have begged to differ with her on that score.

'I really ought to be leaving,' Jake was saying now as he smiled across the table at her and thanked her for the meal. 'I'm expecting a couple of faxes through and—'

'Another multi-million-pound deal,' David interrupted with a grin. 'You'll have to be careful, Jake,' he warned him teasingly, 'otherwise you're going to be a multimillionaire by the time you're forty and then you'll have every fortune-hunter in the district after you...'

'I'm *never* going to be a multimillionaire whilst I've got the estate to finance,' Jake told him truthfully.

'What would you have done if you'd inherited it without the back-up of the money you made during your days in the city trading in shares?' David asked him.

'I don't know; I'd probably have had to sell it. Hopefully one day it will become self-sufficient—the woodlands we've planted will bring in some income when they're mature and with the farming income and subsidies...'

'It would have been a shame if you'd had to sell it,' Janey told him. 'After all, the estate has been in your family for almost two hundred years...'

'Yes, I know...'

'Well, it's high time you were thinking about providing the next generation of little Carlisles if you intend to *keep* it in the family,' David teased him. 'You're not getting any younger, you know; you'll be—what...thirty-four this time...?'

'Thirty-two,' Jake told him dryly. 'I'm a year older than you are...which reminds me, wasn't it Lucianna's birthday last week?'

'Yes,' Janey agreed, adding, 'I rather think she was hoping for an engagement ring from John before he went away to Canada.'

'How's her business doing?' Jake asked Janey, making no response to her comment about Lucianna's disappointed hopes of a birthday proposal.

'Well, she's slowly building up a loyal clientele,' Janey told him cautiously. 'Female drivers in the main, who appreciate having their car serviced by another woman—'

'She's still heavily in debt to the bank,' David broke in forthrightly. 'No man worth his salt would let a woman service his car; we tried to tell her that, but would she listen? No way. It's just as well she's still living here and didn't take on the extra financial burden of renting her own place as she originally wanted to do...'

'You really are a dreadful chauvinist, David,' Janey criticised mildly. 'And whilst we're on the subject Lucianna is, after all, very much what your father and the rest of you have made her. Poor girl, she's never been given much of a chance to develop her femininity, has she?'

CHAPTER TWO

'JOHN got off safely, then?' Janey asked Lucianna cautiously.

They were both in the kitchen, Janey baking and Lucianna poring over her business accounts.

'Only we didn't hear you come in last night,' Janey persisted, waiting until Lucianna had finished adding up the column of figures she was working on before speaking again.

'No... I...I was later than I expected,' Lucianna agreed quietly without looking up, not wanting to admit to her sister-in-law that after John's flight had taken off she had felt so low that instead of driving straight home she had simply wandered aimlessly around the terminal. The brief, almost brotherly kiss John had placed on her forehead before leaving her and the speed with which he had responded eagerly to the very first call for his flight had contrasted painfully with the appreciative and lingering look she had seen him give the attractively dressed woman who had evidently been joining his flight, leaving her painfully aware that despite the fact that they had been dating for several months John seemed more interested in another woman than he was in her.

'Perhaps when John comes home he'll realise how much he's missed you,' Janey began comfortingly, but suddenly Lucianna had had enough. What was the point in pretending to anyone else when she couldn't even pretend to herself any longer? Dolefully, she shook her head, refusing to be comforted.

She and John had originally met six months earlier when John's car had broken down, leaving him stranded a couple of miles from the farm where Lucianna had been brought up and where she now lived with her brother David and his wife Janey.

She had happened to drive past and, recognising John's plight, she had stopped and offered to help, quickly tracking down the problem and cheerfully assuring John that she could soon fix it.

She had first developed her skill with engines as a young girl tinkering with the farm's mechanical equipment—on a farm a piece of equipment that didn't work cost money, and all of the Stewart family had a working knowledge of how to fix a broken-down tractor, but for some reason Lucianna had excelled at almost being able to sense what was wrong even before her older brothers.

This skill had proved to be an asset in her teens when her second eldest brother Lewis had become interested in stock-car racing. Lucianna had happily allowed both Lewis and his friends to make use of her skills in helping them to repair and, in some cases, rebuild their cars.

Because she was the youngest of the family, and had the added handicap of being a girl, she had grown up sensitively aware of the fact that she had to find some way of compensating for the fact that she wasn't a boy and that because of that, in the eyes of her family, she was somehow less worthwhile as a human being.

Unsure of what she wanted to do when she left school, she had continued with her farm chores and increasingly become responsible for not just the maintenance of the farm's machinery but also for the maintenance of several of her brothers' friends' cars, and it had seemed a natural step to move from working with cars as a hobby to working with them as a means of earning a living.

Initially her ambition had been to train and work with some of the top-of-the-range luxury models, but each distributor she had approached with a view to an apprenticeship had laughed at the very idea of a female mechanic and it had been her father who had ultimately suggested she could use one of the empty farm buildings and set up her own business from there.

John had, at first, been shocked and then, she suspected, a little ashamed by the way she earned her living, considering it 'unfeminine'.

Femininity, as she had quickly discovered, was an asset both prized and praised by John and one she did not possess.

Unhappily, she bit her lip. One date with John had led to another and then a regular weekly meeting, but not as yet to the declaration of love and long-term commitment she had been hoping for.

'If he really cared, he'd have…' she began, speaking her painful thoughts out loud before shaking her head, unable to continue. Then she asked Janey tiredly in a low voice. 'What's *wrong* with me, Janey? Why can't I make John see how good we'd be together?'

Lucianna was sitting with her back to the door, and whilst she had been speaking David and Jake had walked across the farmyard and entered the kitchen just in time to hear her low-voiced query.

It was left to Jake to fill the awkward silence left

by her subdued question as he announced, 'Perhaps because he isn't a combustion engine and human relationships need a bit more know-how to make them work than anything you're likely to learn on a basic mechanics course.'

The familiar razor-sharp voice had Lucianna spinning round, hot, angry colour mantling her cheeks, her green eyes flashing with temper, the off-the-face style in which she kept her long, naturally curly hair emphasising her high cheekbones and the stubborn firmness of her chin as she challenged bitterly, 'Who asked you? This is a private conversation and if I'd wanted your opinion, Jake Carlisle…not that I ever would…I'd have asked for it.'

She and Jake had never really got on. Even as a little girl she had disliked and resented his presence in their lives and the influence he seemed to have, not just over her brothers but even over her father as well. Despite the fact that he was only a year older than her eldest brother, there had always been something about Jake that was different, that set him apart from the others—an awareness, a maturity…a certain something which as a child Lucianna had never been able to define but which she only knew made her feel angry…

It had been Jake who had persuaded her aunt to buy her that stupid dress for her thirteenth birthday, the one that had made the boys howl with laughter when they'd seen her in it, the one with the pink frills and sash—the sash which she had later used as binding to tie the wheels of the cart she was making to its chassis. She could still remember the tight-lipped look Jake had given her when he had recognised what it was and the thrill of angry pleasure and defiance it had given her to see that look. Not that he had *said* anything—but then Jake had never needed to say anything to get his message across.

'But you just did,' Jake reminded her, plainly unperturbed by her angry outburst.

'I wasn't talking to *you*, I was talking to Janey,' Lucianna pointed out tersely.

'But perhaps Janey is too kind-hearted to answer you honestly and tell you the truth…'

Lucianna glared at him.

'What truth? What do you mean?'

'You asked what was wrong with you, and why John won't make a commitment to you,' Jake reminded her coolly. 'Well, I'll tell you, shall I? John is a man…not much of one, I'll grant you, but still a man…and, like all heterosexual men, what he wants in his partner…his lover…is a woman. A *woman*, Lucianna—that's spelt W for wantability, O for orgasmic appeal, M for man appeal, A for attraction— sexual attraction, that is—and, of course, finally, N for nuptials. And for your information a woman is someone who knows that the kind of words a man wants to hear whispered in his ear have nothing to do with the latest technical details of a new engine.

'Give me your hand,' he instructed, leaning forward and taking hold of Lucianna's left hand before she could stop him and then studying her ring finger. His long, mobile mouth curled sardonically as he announced, 'Hardly something a man might feel tempted to put his ring on, is it, never mind kiss?'

Mortified, Lucianna snatched her hand away and told him furiously, 'A *woman*…well, I spell it W for wimp, O for obedient, M for moronic, A for artifice and N for nothing…' she told him fiercely.

There was a long silence during which she was uncomfortably conscious of Jake studying her and during which she had to fight to resist the temptation to hide her hands behind her back. Only last weekend she had seen the look of distaste on John's face when he'd complained that her nails weren't long and varnished like those of his friends' girlfriends.

'If that's really how you see yourself, then I feel sorry for you,' Jake declared finally.

It took several seconds for the quiet words to sink in past her turbulent thoughts, but once they had Lucianna blinked and swallowed hard, trying not to cry as the angry, defensive words of denial fought to escape past the hard lump of anguish blocking her throat.

'You aren't a woman, Lucianna,' she heard Jake attack tauntingly into the vulnerability of her silence.

'Yes, I am,' she argued furiously, 'and—'

'No, you're not. Oh, you may look like one, and have all the physical bodily attributes of one—although I must say that given the clothes you choose to shroud yourself in it's hard to know,' he added, with a disparaging glance at the oversized dungarees she was wearing.

'But it isn't looks that make a woman—a real woman—and I'll take a bet that the plainest member of your sex knows more about how to attract than you do... *I* know more...'

'Perhaps you should give Luce a few pointers, then,' David chipped in, laughing. 'Give her a few lessons on how to catch her man...'

'Perhaps I should,' Lucianna heard Jake agreeing thoughtfully, for all the world as though he was seriously considering the matter as some kind of viable, acceptable proposition and not the most ridiculous and insulting thing she had ever heard of in her life!

Lucianna couldn't restrain herself any longer.

'There's nothing you could teach me about being a woman...*nothing*,' she told him defiantly.

'Nothing? Want to bet?' Jake returned smoothly and with dangerous speed. 'You should know better than to challenge *me*, Lucianna. Much better...'

'If I were you I'd take him up on it,' she heard David advising her seriously. 'After all, he *is* a man and—'

'Is he really? Well, thanks for telling me something I didn't know.' Lucianna interrupted her brother with childish sarcasm.

'But you don't know, do you?' Jake slipped in under her defences dulcetly. 'Because you *don't* have very much idea of what a real man actually is, do you, Lucianna?'

'Stop teasing her, both of you,' Janey intervened, adding gently to Lucianna before she could say anything, 'Jake does have a point, though, Luce. And after all with John away for three months it gives you an ideal opportunity to—well, show him when he gets back just exactly what he's been missing,' she concluded lamely, avoiding looking directly at either Lucianna or the two men as she did so.

Lucianna moistened her lips before opening them to tell them in no uncertain terms that they must be mad if they thought she would *ever* entertain such a crazy idea, but no one seemed prepared to listen to her or even to let her speak because Jake was already saying, as though at some point she *had* actually given her verbal agreement to his taunting challenge, 'There'll have to be a few ground rules, of course.'

'Ground rules…' Lucianna glowered at him. 'If by that you mean I'm going to have to take orders from you and…' Then, inexplicably, she had a sudden and very hurtful mental image of that woman she had seen John studying as he'd walked away from her. *Was* it possible? *Could* Jake really show her, teach her…? She swallowed painfully, and to her own disbelief heard herself saying huskily, 'Very well… I agree…'

'My God, you must really want him… Why?'

Underneath the sardonic amusement in Jake's voice ran a fine thread of something else, but Lucianna was too upset to hear it.

'What do you think?' she demanded sharply. 'I love him…'

'I seem to recall you once felt exactly the same about that wreck of a car you insisted on buying— what happened to it by the way?'

'It's still rusting away in the old barn,' David informed him with a grin.

Lucianna gave them both a furious look.

'Right, I want you at the Hall first thing in the morning,' Jake told her. 'Three months may sound a long time but given what we've got to get through… And the first thing you can do—'

'At the Hall? No way. I'm far too busy,' Lucianna told him defiantly.

'Really? That's not what these figures say,' Jake countered, leaning over to study the accounts she had been working on before he'd walked in. 'You're not even breaking even,' he told her.

Lucianna flushed defensively. There was no need for him to point out to her the shortcomings in the financial area of her business; she could see them easily enough for herself, and so too, she imagined, would the bank manager when she next went to see him.

'Of course you're not too busy,' David told her. 'She'll be there, Jake,' he assured his friend. 'Don't you worry.'

Tiredly Lucianna parked her car outside the farmhouse and climbed out. The house itself was in darkness—a sign that David and Janey were already in bed. Their bedroom was at the front of the house, which meant that, hopefully, they wouldn't be disturbed by the security lights springing on at her arrival. She had designed and installed the security system herself, much to David's amusement, and, although the days were gone when she might have expected to find either her father or one of her brothers waiting up to question her late arrival home, farmers and farmers' wives needed their sleep.

She had spent the afternoon with her father. Following his retirement he had moved to a village twenty-odd miles away where he now lived with his widowed elder sister, and Lucianna had promised several days earlier that she would service their ancient Hillman for them. Her mind hadn't really been on the Hillman, though; it had been on Jake Carlisle and his extraordinary challenge, his declaration that he could teach her how to be a woman, the kind of woman men like him—and, according to him, *all* men—really wanted.

Jake, as Lucianna already knew, could be a formidable adversary. It had been Jake, after all, who had persuaded her father to retire when David had given up on ever being allowed to take over and modernise the farm, and Jake who had added the weight of his confidence to her youngest brother Adam's pleas to be allowed to spend time back-packing around the world instead of settling down in a job as her father had wished. Adam was presently working in Australia at a holiday resort on the Barrier Reef.

Dick, the brother between Lewis and Adam in age, was working abroad in China, supervising the building of a new dam, and Lewis was in New York.

What would *they* make of Jake's plan to turn her into a proper woman, the kind of woman John simply couldn't resist? Did she really need to ask herself? First they would roar with laughter and then they would no doubt point out that the task he had taken on was too formidable, too impossible even for his fabled talents.

She wasn't the complete fool her family seemed to think she was, Lucianna assured herself irritably. She knew perfectly well that other young women of her age appeared to have an almost magical ability when it came to attracting the opposite sex that she simply didn't possess, but she refused to believe it was simply a matter of wearing different clothes and adopting the kind of simpering, idiotic manner she suspected that Jake was going to advise her to attempt.

There had been other boys, young men she had dated before she met John, brief friendships which had petered out amicably on both sides, but with John it was different; with John she'd found herself thinking for the first time about a shared future, marriage…children… But, although John always seemed to enjoy her company, so far their relationship had not progressed beyond the odd relatively chaste kiss or affectionate hug.

She had tried to tell herself that John was a gentleman and that he simply didn't want to rush her and she had staunchly held onto that belief until last weekend.

Quietly she let herself into the house and made her way upstairs, pausing on the landing as she heard voices from her brother and sister-in-law's room and then tensing when she realised that she was the subject of their conversation.

She hadn't intended to eavesdrop, she told herself as she recognised that they were discussing the conversation which had taken place in the farmhouse kitchen earlier in the day, but for some reason it was impossible for her to walk away.

'Do you really think Jake's going to be able to teach Lucianna to be more feminine?' she heard Janey asking her husband.

'Not a hope in hell,' she heard David responding cheerfully whilst she held her breath. 'Luce is my sister but, much as I love her, I have to admit that when it comes to sex appeal the poor kid just doesn't have what it takes...'

'Oh, David, that's a bit unkind and unfair,' Janey protested. 'She's got a lovely figure, even if she does hide it behind those dreadful dungarees, and if she paid a little more attention to herself she could be quite stunning. It's not her fault, you know, if all of you treated her like another brother when she was growing up—'

'It doesn't matter what she does,' David interrupted her disparagingly, 'Luce just isn't a man's woman, and not even Jake, despite his experience with the female sex, is going to be able to change that. We might as well face up to the fact that we've got her here on our hands for life...'

Hot tears filled Lucianna's eyes as she crept silently past their bedroom door. Even her own brother thought she was unappealing as a woman. Well, she would show him, she decided angrily. She would show them *all*, and if that meant eating humble pie and taking orders from someone as tirelessly autocratic and bossy as Jake, then despite all the run-ins she had had with him in the past, all the times she had objected to him taking a far too older-brotherly and interfering interest in her life, so be it.

And, loath though she was to admit it, even in the privacy of her own thoughts, she could certainly have no better tutor. She had, after all, had ample opportunity over the years to witness for herself just exactly what effect Jake had on the susceptible and, it had to be admitted, not so susceptible members of her own sex, and, puzzlingly, so far as she could discern, without him apparently having to make any obvious attempts to engage their besotted adoration.

Personally, she couldn't fathom just what it was they saw in him that reduced normally intelligent, witty, independent women to drooling, speechless wrecks; she had never found anything remotely attractive in his black-browed, autocratic and, in her eyes, often censorious maleness. She preferred men like John—fair-haired, kind-eyed men who looked more like cuddly teddy bears than something reminiscent of an adman's image of a truly awesomely male hunk.

She was under no illusions about how unpleasant and unpalatable she was likely to find the entire exercise, nor how much amusement Jake was all too likely to derive from it—at her expense. But enough was enough, and *she* had had enough and more.

Determinedly she brushed away her tears and told herself a second time that it would all be worth it to have John standing lovingly at her side, his ring on her finger.

Five minutes later, in her own room, she paused in the automatic act of getting undressed and walked hesitantly across the room to stand in front of her bedroom mirror.

Only this afternoon her aunt had commented on how like her mother she looked. Her mother had been considered something of a beauty, but wasn't beauty supposed to be in the eyes of the beholder? And she had seen the way John had winced when he had called round unexpectedly earlier in the week, a look of distaste crossing his face as he'd looked at her oil-stained hands and short nails. But John had thought her attractive enough when they had first met and he had been glad enough of her mechanical expertise then too, even proud of it, boasting to his friends about her skill.

It had been later that he had stopped telling others how she earned her living and then, latterly, cautioned her against doing so herself, growing both uncomfortable and irritated with her when she had asked him why.

She knew she was different from the girlfriends and wives of John's friends, and on the thankfully rare occasions when she had been alone with them she had discovered that they very quickly ran out of things to talk about. But what had been even worse, even more humiliating than their silence, had been the laughter she had heard and which had been quickly stifled as she'd walked back into the room after leaving it for a few minutes. She had been in no doubt that they had been talking about her, laughing about her, and that knowledge had hurt even though she had vowed not to let them know it.

At school she had been popular enough and had had plenty of friends, although it was true that once she had reached her teens she had tended to disdain the giggly, boy-focused discussions of her fellow females and spent more time instead with the boys, preferring tomboyish pursuits to long discussions about the latest pop groups or clothes fad.

She had tried, though, with John, really tried. At his suggestion she had bought a new dress for his firm's annual do and she had even gone along with his insistence that she take one of his female colleagues from work along with her to choose it.

And, although she had felt too upset at the time to tell him so, the dress she had so unhappily and unsuccessfully worn had not been her choice but Felicity's. And she still couldn't understand why Felicity had so determinedly and blatantly lied about that fact, insisting in the face of John's disapproval that she, Lucianna, had overridden her advice and chosen her dress herself.

Her eyes filled with fresh tears now—widely spaced, thick-lashed, pretty silvery green eyes which recently had held a far more sombre expression than suited them. It hurt more than she felt able to say to anyone that even her family seemed to think she was somehow lacking in female allure.

Outwardly she might wear jeans and do what appeared to be an unfeminine job, but inwardly... Inwardly, she was every bit as much a woman as the Felicitys of this world, every bit as worthy of being loved and wanted—and she was going to prove it!

CHAPTER THREE

'YOU'RE up early this morning… Not had a change of heart, have you, and planning to do a disappearing act?'

Lucianna shook her head as she listened to her brother's teasing comments.

'Certainly not,' she told him firmly, but he was closer to the truth than he knew. She had woken up this morning with a very heavy heart indeed and a deep and gloomy sense of foreboding and dismay at what she had let herself in for.

'Pull the other one,' her brother advised her, showing that he knew her rather better than she liked and informing Janey as she walked into the kitchen, 'I told you she wouldn't go through with it; she's—'

'I *am* going through with it,' Lucianna interrupted him indignantly. 'I just got up earlier than normal because I want to finish a job off before…before I drive over to…'

To prove a point she gulped down her coffee and started to hurry towards the back door before David could make any further teasing remarks. With her back to him she didn't see the look of compassionate sympathy he gave her before exchanging a rueful glance with his wife.

She was his kid sister, damn it, and he loved her, and he could wring that idiot John's neck for the misery he was causing her.

The job Lucianna had pretended was so urgent was

simply a matter of changing an oil filter, and she was on her way back to the house when Jake drove into the farmyard.

'What are *you* doing here?' she challenged him aggressively as he got out of his car. Like her he was casually dressed in jeans, but unlike hers his were immaculately clean and they fitted him properly.

'What do you think?' he retorted calmly.

Lucianna gave him a stubborn look.

'There's no need for you to come and collect me as if I were a…a prisoner. I was going to drive myself over…'

'But now I've saved you the trouble,' Jake told her suavely, 'and that's one of the first lessons you have to learn.'

'What?' Lucianna asked.

'How to accept a man's naturally chivalrous instinct to look after and protect a woman—and,' he added more dryly, 'how not to dent his ego by pointing out that you don't need or want his protection.'

'How? By simpering stupidly and throwing myself at your feet in gratitude?' Lucianna demanded acidly.

'A simple "thank you" and a warm smile would be perfectly adequate. You want to thank the guy, not make him think you're desperate,' Jake told her.

Lucianna glowered at him whilst she felt her face grow hot with indignation.

'I am *not* desperate—' she began, but Jake was already shaking his head, telling her directly,

'Don't give me that, Luce… I know you, remember, and for you to go to such lengths…'

'I *love* him,' she told him, tilting her chin determinedly at him as though daring him to argue with her.

'You might think you do but, believe me, you don't even begin to know what love is yet.'

Her brother's emergence into the yard prevented Lucianna from making the kind of retort she wanted to make but she was still seething with resentment and indignation ten minutes later as she sat next to Jake whilst he reversed his car back out of the yard.

'Your timing's out,' she told him critically as she listened to the sound of the engine.

'You're going to have to know me a lot better before you can come out with a comment like that,' he told her in an unfamiliar soft and meaningful voice that made her turn her head and look open-mouthed at him as her senses, more acute and finely tuned than her brain, recognised a message in the dulcet, husky sound of his voice that her brain could not quite pick up on.

'*My* timing is *never* out,' he added even more softly, and then reverted to his normal tone of voice, before she could say anything, to tell her briskly, 'But yes, the *car's* timing is slightly out, Lucianna...

'Tell me something,' he went on conversationally. 'When you and John are alone what do you talk about?'

'Talk about?' Lucianna stared at him.

'You *do* talk, I take it?' Jake questioned dryly. 'Or is your main form of communication on a, shall we say, more basic level?'

It took several seconds for what he meant to sink in, but once it had done Lucianna could feel her face beginning to burn with a mixture of fury and embarrassment.

'Of *course* we talk,' she snapped. 'We talk about all kinds of things...'

'Such as?' Jake demanded, one dark eyebrow raised interrogatively, the profile he was angling slightly towards her uncomfortably reminiscent of the stern demeanour with which he had lectured her on some of her youthful follies.

'Er…lots of things,' Lucianna told him, desperately hunting through her memory for suitably impressive examples of the breadth and erudition of their shared conversations.

'Really? So you'd agree with those who claim that verbal foreplay can be just as erotic and arousing as its physical equivalent, then, would you?' Jake asked her.

'Verbal foreplay!' Lucianna's colour deepened. 'John and I have far better things to talk about than sex,' she snapped bitingly.

'*And* better things to do?'

The soft question slipped very subtly and, yes, sneakily beneath her guard, leaving her totally unable to come up with any safe response other than a taut, 'I don't discuss such personal things with anyone!'

But even that defence could not protect her, as she quickly discovered when Jake unkindly suggested, 'Not even John? You might be able to strip down an engine very effectively and efficiently, Lucianna, but somehow or other I doubt that you have the same skill when it comes to stripping down a man—or *for* a man,' he added with dangerous softness.

Struggling to overcome her mortification, Lucianna stared fixedly ahead through the car windscreen. Little did Jake know it but his scathing remark had echoed an unkind conversation she had recently overheard between two of John's friends—girlfriends.

'Can you imagine it?' one had said to the other,

unaware that Lucianna could hear them. 'She'll be saying to John, ''Now this bit goes here and then this bit goes there and then you have to do this.'' Poor John, I feel so sorry for him. I can't understand what he sees in her, can you?'

Perhaps her sexual experience wasn't all that extensive—at least not in the practical sense—and perhaps, yes, she did rather quail at the thought of having to take the sexual initiative with a man—certainly she had never or *would* never have attempted to undress one. But she could read, and if John had been rather slow to pick up on her hesitant signals that she was ready to take their relationship a few steps further than the kisses and caresses they had so far shared then she had at least, until recently, put it down to the fact that he valued and respected her and their relationship enough to let the sexual side of things develop slowly and naturally. After all, the last thing she wanted was to be wanted merely for sex.

She frowned, suddenly realising that whilst she had been deep in thought Jake had been driving them not towards his home but along the road that led into town instead.

'Where are we going?' she demanded sharply. 'I thought—'

'I'm taking you shopping,' Jake informed her calmly.

'Shopping?' Lucianna tensed, warily remembering all the occasions on which her family had attempted to persuade her to change her style of dress. She knew they thought she was being stubborn and difficult in refusing to listen to what they had to say, but how could she tell them that her refusal to abandon her dungarees and jeans had its roots a long way back in her early teenage years?

Then, as a young schoolgirl, she had desperately wanted to look like her female peers and not like the tomboy she had heard others disparagingly call her.

The gift of some birthday money had given her the opportunity to turn her wishes into reality and she could still remember the excitement with which she had gone shopping with another girl from school, a girl who, in her then youthful and untutored eyes, had seemed to have all the feminine attributes she herself so longed for.

She still shuddered to recall what had followed when, dressed up in her new purchases—the uncomfortable suspender belt and stockings, the tight short skirt and the high heels that had made her wobble perilously as she'd walked nervously at her friend's side—they had encountered a group of boys from school.

The crude remarks which had followed her transformation from tomboy into a girl who they had plainly believed was making herself sexually available had made her ears and her face burn for weeks and months afterwards, her embarrassment and sense of shame so great that she had actually refused to go to school the following week until her father had announced that he was sending for the doctor.

The incident, coupled with her own brothers' derogatory comments about a certain type of girl, had so shocked and shamed her that she had never worn the clothes again, and in the years since, although in her wardrobe there were several rather more formal outfits than her preferred dress of dungarees and jeans, she had steadfastly refused to give in to her family's exhortations to buy or wear 'something feminine'. She had experienced already what happened when she did that, how the male sex reacted, knew that for some reason which was not really clear to herself there was something about her that made it impossible for her to wear the kind of clothes other women wore with such ease and confidence without cheapening herself and making herself an object of sexual contempt and ridicule.

'I'm not going,' Lucianna suddenly announced tersely. 'Stop the car.'

Calmly Jake did so, but the atmosphere inside the car felt anything but calm as he turned to her and asked her critically, 'What is it you're so afraid of, Lucianna? And don't try to deny that you are; I know you—remember? Are you frightened of failure—failing to be enough woman to—?'

'No...'

'No?' One dark eyebrow rose in the interrogative and superior manner she was so familiar with and which so irritated her. 'Then prove it,' Jake suggested quietly.

'I don't need to prove *anything* to you,' Lucianna told him angrily.

'Not to me, no,' Jake agreed, overriding her angry words, 'but you certainly seem to have something to prove to John—and to yourself.'

Lucianna looked away from him, unable to meet his eyes and unable to refute his statement.

'It's your choice,' he told her evenly, 'your decision, but I must say you've surprised me...'

'Surprised you!'

Lucianna gave him a wary look. In her experience surprising Jake took an awful lot of doing.

'Mmm…' he agreed, nodding. 'I thought you had more courage, more guts…more self-respect than to give up without at least making some attempt to fight for what you want.'

'I do have,' Lucianna retorted indignantly, and then added truculently, 'Oh, very well, then, but if you think I'm going to let you bully me into wasting money on some stupid, silly outfit that *you* think a woman should wear—'

'Excuse me, but whilst I may have been guilty of many sins in my time, Lucianna, wanting to see a woman dressed in frills isn't one of them. And besides, you're a long, long way yet from being ready to change your outer image… It's your inner image we're going to be working on today and for many days to come.

'Femininity, womanliness, is something that comes from within. It means being proud of yourself as a woman, being confident about your femaleness and your sexuality; it's showing the world that you value yourself *as* a woman… When a person has that, how they choose to *clothe* their body is really immaterial apart from the fact that what they choose to wear acts like a shorthand message to those who see her.'

Whilst he'd been talking he had restarted the car, and this time Lucianna made no objection as he continued to drive towards the town.

Something about the calm way he had delivered those few unexpected words had for some odd reason or other brought a huge uncomfortable lump of emotion to her throat, an indefinable sense of loss and sorrow, as though he had highlighted something within her which she had secretly felt had never been allowed to flourish and had even more secretly hidden away in shame even from herself.

Yet as she sat silently at his side her thoughts, unexpectedly, were not of herself or even of John but, surprisingly, of her mother.

Might not things have been different if she had not died when Lucianna was so young…? Might not *she* have been different?

'But this is a book shop,' Lucianna protested as Jake determinedly ushered her through the plate-glass doors.

They had arrived in the town five minutes earlier and, having parked the car, Jake had directed her towards the town's main shopping street.

'That's right,' Jake agreed, touching her lightly on the arm as he pointed to a labelled section of books on the far side of the shop. 'I think we'll find what we need over there,' he told her.

Lucianna frowned; the shelves seemed to be filled with diet and self-improvement books so far as she could see. Warily she allowed Jake to propel her in their direction.

'I don't think these will be of much benefit to me,' she told him as she studied the title of the diet book which was prominently displayed.

'I doubt it,' he agreed. 'If anything you need to put weight on.'

'To make me more feminine?' Lucianna suggested, her hackles starting to rise at his implied criticism of her.

'To make you more *healthy*,' Jake corrected her. 'You're naturally fine-boned and delicate—anyone can see that,' he added, startling her as he totally unexpectedly ran his index finger along the curve of her cheekbone, producing an aftershock of sensation on her skin in the wake of his touch something like the kind of feeling she associated with an unexpected rash of goosebumps but with an extra indefinable and unfamiliar something which made her feel peculiarly light-headed and breathless.

'And it naturally follows that your body will be similarly delicately made, long-legged and high-breasted with a narrow waist,' he told her, emphasising his point by reaching out and placing his hands at either side of her body.

Her indignant verbal objection was never uttered as she looked down at where his thumbs met and felt the hard, warm male pressure of his grip through the thickness of her clothes. A suffocating tightness had invaded her chest, far, far tighter and more constricting, more dangerous than Jake's firm grip on her body.

'I can't breathe,' she protested angrily and huskily, reaching out to take hold of his arms as she instinctively tried to force him to release her.

'Can't you?'

The most peculiar and disturbing sensation she had ever experienced in her life seized her as she heard the deeper note in Jake's voice and felt her whole body trembling uncontrollably in response to it in some secret inner vibration. When she looked at him she discovered that his gaze seemed to be focused on her mouth. Probably because he was waiting for her angry objection to his behaviour, she told herself protectively as she fought to control a sudden compulsive need to wet her almost painfully dry lips with the tip of her tongue—and lost.

'Stop it,' she hissed breathlessly. 'Stop it at once…'

'Stop what?' Jake responded mock innocently.

'You know perfectly well what. Stop looking at my…at me like…like you were doing,' she finished lamely, her colour high as she thankfully felt him respond to her agitation and lift his head to meet her eyes at the same time as he removed his hands from her waist.

'You're looking very hot and bothered; what's wrong?' he asked her, outwardly solicitously, but she could see the laughter gleaming in his eyes.

'You know perfectly well what's wrong,' she told him forthrightly. 'It's you…the way you…the way you looked at me.'

'You mean the way a man looks at a woman he wants,' Jake told her calmly. 'It's called body language,' he continued, before Lucianna could take issue with him on the first part of his statement. 'The way a man looks at a woman he wants'—indeed! Well, she knew one thing and that was that he certainly *didn't* want her—and she would never *want* him to want her, she added hastily. It was John she wanted to want her, to desire her, to love her.

'Body language,' Jake repeated instructively as he reached up and removed a couple of books from higher up the shelves and handed them to her. He explained, 'It's a fact that all of us both consciously and subconsciously send out messages to others with every movement we make, every expression we show, and the first step to getting others to be responsive is for you to show them that you are open to that responsiveness.

'For example, just now when I looked at your

mouth, you touched your lips with your tongue, which means—'

'Which means that you were making me nervous and angry.'

'Nervous?' Jake queried with a small half-smile that made her look warily away from him.

'Nervous and angry,' she insisted, but she knew that her voice didn't sound quite as convincing and determined as she would have liked.

'Mmm... I see. So when John looks at your mouth like that what kind of response do you give him?' he asked her placatingly, but Lucianna was too on edge to be placated.

'John *never* looks at me like that,' she answered quickly.

She only realised her mistake when Jake said softly, 'Oh, dear. Well, I'm sure there'll be some advice inside these—' he tapped the books. '—to indicate how you can rectify that situation, and if there isn't—well, I can always...'

But Lucianna wasn't listening. Snatching the books from his hand, she headed determinedly towards the till, head held high as the salesgirl gave the titles a quick, curious glance before taking Lucianna's money and putting them into a bag for her.

'I know her—I serviced her mother's car,' Lucianna hissed angrily to Jake once they were outside the shop. 'I suppose you think all this is very funny,' she added crossly as she fished the books out of the carrier bag, and she read the titles to him in scornful disgust. *'The Science of Body Language and How to Use it Effectively*, and *The Art of Flirtation.'*

'Funny?' Jake repeated. 'No, Lucianna,' he told her curtly. 'I don't think *any* of this is *remotely* funny.'

He looked so grim and unapproachable that the demand to know just what he did think of it and her, which she had been about to voice, died unvoiced.

'This way,' he told her, touching her, indicating the pretty town square which lay ahead of them. Set out with trees and benches and with the sun shining warmly, it was obviously a popular spot with office workers for eating their sandwiches.

One couple were vacating one of the benches as they approached and Jake quickly appropriated the spare seats.

'What now?' Lucianna asked wearily as he indicated that he wanted to sit down.

'Now we're going to do a bit of people-watching,' Jake told her. 'Let's see just how sharp and accurate your instincts actually are and at the same time let's see how much visual experience of the art of body language you can actually recognise.'

'It wasn't called that. It was called *The Art of Flirtation*,' Lucianna snapped back at him.

'Same thing,' Jake told her dryly. 'Now,' he commanded sternly once Lucianna had reluctantly seated herself beside him, 'take a good look around and tell me what you can see.'

Lucianna took a deep breath and mentally counted to ten before telling him irritably, 'I can see the town square and part of the high street and I can see—'

'That wasn't what I meant, Lucianna,' Jake interrupted her crisply, the look in his eyes as he turned to study her the same one he had used to reinforce his older and male status during the years when she had been growing up.

Then it had quelled her and even sometimes made her feel warily apprehensive and, as she now discovered to her chagrin, things hadn't changed all that much. The only difference was that now she felt seriously tempted to ignore his visual warning and see what just *might* happen. After all, what could he really do if she simply got up and walked away?

As though he had read her mind he advised her sharply, 'I wouldn't if I were you. You agreed to this, remember. You're the one who's desperate to prove—'

'I'm not *desperate* to prove *anything*,' Lucianna argued hotly.

'Do you know something, Lucianna?' Jake said wryly. 'Your determination to win John rather reminds me of the same blind stubbornness that a child exhibits in demanding a sweet or a toy simply because it's out of reach and being denied them, and I can't help wondering if it's the fact that he seems out of reach that makes him seem so desirable. There certainly doesn't seem—'

'I'm not a child,' Lucianna began, then realised how neatly and easily she had fallen into the trap Jake had dug for her as he told her sharply,

'No? Well, then, I suggest you cease behaving like one. Now, look around again and tell me what you see, and this time study the people—carefully. Look at that group over there just coming out of the chemist's, for instance, and tell me what you see.'

Heaving a deep sigh, Lucianna painstakingly and dutifully stared in the direction he had indicated.

A man and a woman and two small children were standing on the pavement just outside the chemist's. The woman was leaning towards the man and smiling up at him. The two children were dancing up and down beside them, obviously excited, whilst the man started to remove some papers from his pocket.

At the same time the woman instinctively reached out to draw the children closer to her as a car drove past and the man put out a hand to steady *her* as another shopper looked as though she might barge into them.

They were obviously a family, Lucianna could see that, and a happy one, she acknowledged as she saw their smiles and heard their laughter as they all looked at the strips of photographs the man was holding, the two children barely able to contain their excitement.

But stubbornly she omitted to mention anything of this as she responded to Jake's instruction by simply saying, 'I see a man, a woman and two children.'

'You're beginning to try my patience, Lucianna,' Jake warned her. 'Look again. Look at the way the man is behaving towards the three of them—protectively, lovingly—and the way the woman is responding to *him*, the way she obviously feels that *he's* done something special; and the two children—look at their excitement.

'At a guess I would say that they are a young couple who are just planning their first continental holiday with their children and that they have just been to obtain their family passport photographs. This holiday is probably something they've planned for and saved for for a very long time, something they've had to make sacrifices to afford, especially the man who's probably had to work extra hours to pay for it...'

'That's sexist,' Lucianna objected. 'It might be the woman who's had to do the extra work.'

'It's not sexist at all,' Jake denied. 'I'm simply interpreting their body language. Look at the way the man's almost preening himself. Look at the way the woman's looking at him, the pride and love in her expression, the way she keeps looking at him and touching his arm, and look at the way he's responding. An animal psychologist would probably say they're simply copying an ancient grooming ritual from the animal kingdom and that the one lower down the pecking order is grooming the ones higher up it, so that in this particular instance I would guess that it is the man who's earned the extra money.

'But he's obviously a modern father; look at the way he's bending down now to fasten the elder child's shoes and the way she's leaning against him. It's obvious that fastening her shoes is a task he's comfortably familiar with, just as she's obviously comfortably familiar with him—'

'Very interesting, but I can't really see its relevance for me,' Lucianna interrupted him crossly. Suddenly, for some reason, the sight of the small, happy family was making her feel acutely aware of her own aloneness. 'After all, *I'm* not likely to want to start fastening John's shoes or grooming him,' she added sarcastically.

'You might not want to fasten his shoes,' Jake agreed, 'but as for grooming... It's normally considered to be an important and enjoyable part of the human courting ritual—to touch and be touched, to exchange those but oh, so meaningful caresses... Or am I being old-fashioned? Sex has been stripped of so much of its allure and sensuality these days.

'It's almost as though the race towards orgasm has become a fast-paced motorway requiring intense concentration and a total focus on reaching one's goal, with no opportunity or desire to enjoy the pleasure of a more leisurely meander that allows one to pause and enjoy the moment, the caress.

'Is that what *you* prefer, Lucianna—a sensible, no-nonsense approach to sex that reduces it simply to a biological urge which needs to be satisfied in the most efficient and least time-consuming manner?'

'How I think and feel about sex has *nothing* to do with this *nor* with you,' Lucianna told him fiercely.

'No? Well, if that's what you think no wonder you're having so much trouble. On the contrary, sex has *everything* to do with it—or it should do. When you look at John, if you don't want him to reach out and touch you and if you don't want to reach out and touch him, then—'

'John *never* touches me in public,' Lucianna interrupted him, her colour rising as she told him angrily, 'And nor would I want him to.'

'Well, you certainly should,' Jake told her, as calm as she herself was becoming flustered as he suddenly turned towards her and before she could stop him reached out and curled his fingers around her bare wrist.

His grip, although light, disturbed her. She could feel her heart start to beat faster with what she told herself was anger at his high-handed manner and her pulse was certainly racing because Jake himself was now placing his thumb over it, as though aware of her tension, his thumb beginning a slow, rhythmic stroking of the inside of her wrist which she assumed must be intended to calm and relax her but which, instead, was sending her heartbeat into a crazy, irregular volley of frantic thuds which were matched by the dizzying acceleration of her pulse. No wonder she was finding it difficult to breathe, she told herself hazily.

Through the ragged sound of her own breathing she could hear Jake telling her softly, 'I'm touching you now, Lucianna; I'm touching you the way a man, a lover, the way *John* should want to touch you in public as an indication of his desire to touch you more intimately in private.'

Through the confused jumble of messages assaulting her sensory system Lucianna's brain managed to isolate and hold onto one of them.

'But you aren't John,' she reminded Jake breathlessly.

'No,' he agreed, his stroking thumb suddenly ceasing its inflammatory circular movement against her skin and his voice hardening slightly. 'And I promise you that if I were you would be in no doubt as to *my* feelings for you, Lucianna...'

'I'm not,' she managed to find the robustness to say. 'I do know exactly how you feel about me, Jake,' she told him, and then added succinctly, 'And I promise you I feel exactly the same way about you, only more so.'

Some feminine instinct made her tilt her head determinedly as she threw the words at him, but the look of blazing heat in his eyes as he gazed back at her made her look away again hastily.

She had never seen him look so...so...passionate...so...intense. Normally he was such a calm, controlled man. Too calm and controlled—aggravatingly so at times.

'Luc.'

She turned her head, frowning slightly as she recognised the voice of John's colleague, Felicity. She didn't particularly like Felicity especially since the shopping debacle. She was a tall, leggy brunette with a faintly supercilious manner and a habit of shortening Lucianna's name and pronouncing it as though indeed she had been christened as a boy in the same slightly patronising, sneering manner she was using now.

'Have you heard anything from John yet?' she asked Lucianna, speaking to her but plainly far more visually interested in concentrating on Jake, at whom she was smiling.

Somehow or other she'd managed to stand so that she was facing Jake, keeping her body half turned away from Lucianna, effectively excluding her, and had placed herself closer to Jake than Lucianna herself was. She added, 'We had a fax from him this morning saying that he's settled in safely but that he's missing us.'

'Yes, he faxed me as well,' Lucianna heard herself fibbing, much to her own surprise and shock.

It must be something to do with the lecture Jake had just been giving her about observing other people's body language that was making her so crossly aware of the unsubtle manoeuvres Felicity was using to attempt to create an aura of intimacy between herself and Jake which totally excluded Lucianna.

Well, let her. Let *them*, she decided angrily. She didn't care and it was typical of Jake that he should have attracted Felicity's attention. He was that kind of man.

'Are you one of Luc's customers?' she heard Felicity questioning Jake, her voice low and musical, her laughter a soft feminine gurgle as she added depreciatingly, 'I think she's wonderful doing what she does. To my shame I have to admit I don't even know how to change a tyre...'

'It isn't the tyre you change, it's the wheel,' Lucianna informed her shortly. She stood up and said pointedly to Jake, 'I thought you said we were going shopping...'

'Shopping? Now that is something I *do* know about,' Felicity enthused.

For one appalling moment Lucianna thought that she was going to have to suffer the additional humiliation of hearing Jake invite Felicity to join them, but to her relief he simply smiled at her instead and then turned towards Lucianna, placing his hand beneath her elbow as he rose, and standing firmly close to her.

If someone had told her ten minutes ago that she would actually be grateful to have Jake display such old-fashioned male courtesy and protectiveness towards her she would have denied it with scorn, so it was just as well someone hadn't, because if they had right now she would have been eating her own words, she admitted uncomfortably.

Jake waited until they were out of Felicity's earshot before saying smoothly, 'You never said anything about John getting in touch with you.'

'I don't tell you everything,' Lucianna returned. Jake was still lightly holding her arm, but when she tried to pull away from him she discovered that his hold on her was much firmer than she had imagined and rather than subject herself to an undignified tussle of physical strength which she knew he would win she had to satisfy herself with glowering at him and a brief and, although she didn't know it, betrayingly feminine toss of her head that made Jake fight to hide a rueful smile.

He pointed out dryly, 'Evidently not. Like you didn't tell me you'd acquired a fax machine.'

'Oh!' Lucianna couldn't manage to control the stricken look that crossed her face as he reminded her of the lie she had told Felicity. 'Well, I couldn't let her think that John had got in touch with his office and not me,' she defended herself.

'The office or her?' Jake questioned cynically, and then, to Lucianna's astonishment, he raised his free hand and touched her cheekbone lightly with his thumb as though he were brushing away some dirt or a tear, before saying softly, 'Well, your feminine instincts are there all right. Now let's see if we can unearth a few more of them. When did you last wear something that wasn't a pair of jeans or dungarees, Lucianna?'

'Last night,' she told him smartly as she fought to get back the breath that had suddenly deserted her when he'd touched her face with such mock tenderness. As his eyebrows rose she added sweetly, 'I don't sleep in my work clothes, Jake.'

'No, you sleep in a cotton nightdress,' he agreed sardonically. 'The same one you've been wearing since you were fifteen years old, I imagine.'

'It's still cold at night,' she protested, feeling her face starting to heat up at the taunting note in his voice. 'I like to curl my feet up into it...'

'A woman in love...a woman *with* a lover... wouldn't need a nightdress to keep her warm,' Jake told her mockingly, adding hurtfully, 'But then *you* aren't a woman, are you, Lucianna? Not yet...'

'Not according to you,' she agreed, driven recklessly to answer him back to make him stop taunting her, and she added, 'What's wrong, Jake? Are you having second thoughts, beginning to feel that you've taken on too much, that you can't transform me after all…make me a woman…?'

The look that crossed his face, the utter stillness of his body whilst his eyes turned dark and hot with an emotion she couldn't recognise made her tense warily, not sure what it was she had said or done to unleash the fury she could sense he was trying to control, only knowing that she had suddenly and frighteningly strayed into an area of his personality she wasn't familiar with.

'Don't tempt me,' she heard him saying softly to her. 'Just don't tempt me, Lucianna.'

Don't tempt him to what? she wondered shakily as his hand dropped from her arm as though her skin had burned him. Don't tempt him to wring her neck, probably, she decided unhappily, forced to increase her stride to try to keep up with him as he strode down the street.

Scowling darkly, she flirted momentarily with the idea of telling him that she had changed her mind and that she didn't want or need his help after all, but then she remembered the triumphant mockery she had heard in Felicity's voice when she had told her about John's fax and the slanting-eyed come-hither look she had given Jake, the same look Lucianna had seen her giving John on several previous occasions, and her head lifted and her spine straightened.

Jake, who had turned to wait for her to catch up with him, watched her discreetly.

She looked for all the world like a youthful teenager, her slender body encased in oversized clothes, but she wasn't a child, she was an adult, a woman. A woman whose most basic instincts had been aroused by the threat of losing her man.

Her man. Jake's frown returned as he turned abruptly away from Lucianna. The task he had taken on was fraught with innumerable perils, not the least of which was the fact that he might succeed and that Lucianna would get her way—and her man.

CHAPTER FOUR

'WHAT are you looking at?' Lucianna demanded of Jake as he paused on the corner of the street they were entering to watch something, or rather someone. When Lucianna realised she flushed and gave a rather self-conscious, 'Oh,' as she saw the girl Jake had obviously been admiring come sauntering into view.

Like Lucianna she was dressed in jeans, and like her she also had tawny-coloured long hair, but that was where the resemblance between them ended.

Whereas Lucianna's hair was tied back uncompromisingly this girl's was worn loose and slightly messy, giving the impression that she had been doing something far too pleasurable to waste time grooming her hair before coming out, and she had obviously also neglected to put on any proper underwear beneath the neatly fitting cream stretch jeans she was wearing, Lucianna decided scathingly as she saw Jake's glance move from the other girl's face to her body.

There might not be anything openly tarty about the girl's appearance, Lucianna acknowledged, but there was still definitely an air about her and about the way she was dressed that somehow suggested even to Lucianna's inexperienced eye that she was a person who enjoyed her own sexuality.

'Typical.' Lucianna couldn't quite stop herself from saying this disparagingly as she saw the small, teasing look the girl gave Jake before turning away and strolling across the road—or rather sashaying across the road, Lucianna acknowledged—if that wasn't too old-fashioned a word to use for the provocatively swaying movement of the girl's pert bottom.

'Jealous?' Jake asked her mockingly.

'Certainly not,' Lucianna told him scathingly, adding pithily, 'And I wouldn't dream of coming out without my...not wearing any underwear...'

'Not wearing...?' Jake was frowning slightly as he turned to give the girl another brief look, but when he turned back towards her Lucianna could see that he was struggling not to laugh.

'You really do need educating, don't you?' he told her with a grin that made him suddenly look much younger and made her equally suddenly wonder why she was finding it such a struggle to fill her lungs properly with air.

'If being educated means dressing like a...like that, then I'd rather stay the way I am,' she began crossly, but Jake shook his head.

Still laughing, he told her, 'You're wrong, you know. She's more than likely wearing a string of some type underneath her jeans, and—'

'A string...?'

'Yes, you know, an item of underwear...an item of *female* underwear...that is commonly worn beneath fitted clothing to prevent the unforgivable fashion solecism of VPL...'

'VPL...?' Lucianna repeated in irritation.

'Visible panty line,' Jake explained patiently.

'I know what it means,' Lucianna told him. She might not be fashion-conscious, but she *did* read her sister-in-law's magazines and she knew perfectly well what he meant. Her anger was directed not so much at him for teasing her but at herself for giving him the opportunity to do so.

'I take it that it isn't an item of underwear *you* favour?' Jake said to her as they continued to walk down the street.

'My underwear is not something I intend to discuss with you,' Lucianna told him frostily.

'Pity,' Jake returned, his voice suddenly crisply ominous, 'because, much as it pains me to say it, the male of the species, still at heart being the un-newmanish creature that he is, is still very much influenced and intrigued by women's underwear, let's be honest, is perhaps still regrettably prone to making character and personality judgements on a woman based on her choice of underwear and his idea of what he personally finds exciting and erotic...'

'If you're talking about stockings and suspenders...' Lucianna began warily. She had heard more than enough about the allure and potential of such garments from her brothers during the years they were growing up to have been put off wearing them for life.

'Amongst other things,' Jake agreed. 'Personally, what I find erotic is the knowledge that a woman cares enough for herself and for me to want the act of undressing her to become a sensually special appetiser to our loveplay... Rather like the anticipation and buzz one gets from unwrapping an enticingly wrapped present...'

'Oh, you *would* see a woman like that...as a thing...a toy...a...a present...' Lucianna told him furiously. 'Well, for your information, I would rather die than present myself like that...than humiliate and degrade myself like that...'

'So you expect John to enjoy the sight and act of watching you strip down to the utilitarian and functional underwear you no doubt favour, do you? Tell me something, Lucianna,' Jake challenged her. 'Do you permit him to be equally uncompromising with you? Do you enjoy the sight of him wearing a pair of well-washed baggy boxer shorts, or perhaps the gimmicky jockstrap his pals gave him as a joke for his birthday?'

Lucianna's face had gone scarlet, as much with embarrassment as with anger.

'John and I don't have that kind of relationship, and I don't...'

When she stopped Jake demanded with dangerous softness, 'Yes, do go on; you don't what?'

Stubbornly Lucianna pursed her lips and looked away, refusing to speak. She wasn't going to tell Jake that she had no idea what kind of underwear John favoured any more than she was going to admit that the mental images he had just drawn for her, especially the one of John, had somehow or other rung unpalatably true. His pals were the type who would give him jokey and embarrassing underwear as a present.

Jake, on the other hand, would not doubt— Her thoughts careened to an unsteady halt as she abruptly realised that the mental image she had conjured up of Jake's body, superimposed over the image of an unknown model posing in a pair of immaculate pristine white and very close-fitting undershorts that she had glimpsed in an advertisement in one of her sister-in-law's magazines, was one she most certainly should not be entertaining. One she most certainly should not be entertaining at all, and she had no idea exactly why she was—or, even more importantly, how she was.

After all, the last time she had seen Jake without...wearing very little, she amended to herself hastily, had been the last time they had all gone swimming together before Jake had gone to university. And that had been years ago. She had been a child and Jake had been a young man...a boy...whereas the body she had been mentally visualising had most definitely been that of a man...very definitely that of a man.

'Lucianna!'

Self-consciously Lucianna avoided Jake's eyes as she heard the questioning note in his voice.

'Right,' Jake announced, lifting his wrist to glance at his watch. 'That's enough shopping for today. It's time we were making our way back, I think. I've got some work to do and whilst I'm doing it you can make a start with your homework,' he informed her dryly, nodding in the direction of the books she was carrying.

'I can do that by myself at home,' Lucianna told him spiritedly, not in the least relishing the idea of having to sit reading dutifully beneath Jake's eagle eye like a schoolgirl. 'John might ring,' she added.

'So much the better,' Jake retorted firmly. 'It will do him good to wonder where you are. No more excuses, Lucianna,' he advised her. 'Don't forget you wanted to do this...'

Reluctantly Lucianna had to concede that he had a point. There had been moments during the morning, far too many of them in fact, when she had been in danger of forgetting just why she was putting herself through such a painful process.

As they turned into the car park they were greeted

by the shrill sound of a car alarm ringing. To Lucianna's surprise, Jake halted abruptly and cursed under his breath, muttering feelingly, 'If that's what I think it is, that damn garage…'

Lucianna's eyes widened as she stared across the car park and saw that it was indeed Jake's car alarm that was ringing, the car's indicator lights flashing on and off as though someone had tried to break into the vehicle, and she couldn't resist saying dulcetly, 'Oh, dear, Jake, it looks like something has gone wrong with your car's electronics.'

The look Jake gave her told her that he wasn't in the least deceived by her mock-innocent concern.

'*I* don't have a problem,' he told her forcefully, 'but the *garage* is certainly going to have one. They assured me that they'd found the fault and solved the problem.'

'The electronics systems in these expensive status cars are very complicated and sensitive,' Lucianna told him sweetly, with triumph in her voice.

Only six months earlier, when Jake had first taken delivery of his new car, she had begged to be allowed to familiarise herself with its mechanical and electronics systems, but Jake had sternly refused, telling her in what she had considered at the time to be an extremely bossy manner that the car wasn't a toy and that furthermore it would negate its warranty if he allowed anyone who wasn't an approved mechanic to tamper with its inner workings.

'I don't want to tamper with them,' she had told him through gritted teeth. 'I simply want to look at them…'

'I know your looking,' Jake had reminded her grittily. 'I haven't forgotten what happened when you *looked* at the engine of my TR7.'

Lucianna had grimaced. The TR7 had been Jake's pride and joy, a racy little sports car he had worked hard to buy, and just as soon as his back was turned she had ignored his veto on her touching it. He had returned earlier than expected one afternoon when he had been supposed to be away all day to discover her sitting on the floor of his garage, surrounded by the parts she had painstakingly removed from his car.

It hadn't been *her* fault that he had flustered her so much with his ire that she had muddled up two very similar pieces when she had rushed to reassemble everything. Just as soon as she had realised what she had done and why it wouldn't start, why the heating system was throwing out freezing-cold air instead of hot, she had quickly put matters right—but not, as it turned out, quickly enough to repair the damage the shock of icy cold air blasting over Jake's girlfriend's body had done to Jake's budding romance with her.

It wasn't her fault that his girlfriend had chosen to wear such a stupidly short skirt, Lucianna had defended herself, her already hot face growing even hotter when her amused elder brother had hooted with laughter and told Jake teasingly that it was probably the first time his passionate advances had been frozen off by a faulty car heater.

'The first time and the last,' Jake had replied grimly, then had advised Lucianna tersely, 'Don't you ever, ever tamper with my car again, otherwise you'll be the one in need of a blast of cold air—on your backside, which will be smarting very hotly indeed…'

Lucianna had just been at an age when any reference to almost any part of her anatomy had had the power to raise a deeply mortifying crimson flood of colour through her body—and on that occasion, if she remembered aright, her self-consciousness had outdone itself.

Now she watched in secret glee as Jake tried to silence the car's shrilling alarm, first by using the automatic door key and then, once he had got the car unlocked, by deactivating the alarm itself.

'I thought these things were supposed to stop automatically after twenty minutes,' Jake gritted through grated teeth as all his attempts to stop the alarm met with no response.

'That's house alarms,' Lucianna informed him sunnily, her glee growing as she saw the faint tinge of colour beginning to burn his skin. For the first time in the whole of the time she had known him, Jake was actually beginning to exhibit the tell-tale signs of becoming harassed. His hair was rumpled where he had pushed his hand through it and she could see from his expression that he wasn't enjoying the attention and pity they were attracting from other motorists.

'It could be worse,' she comforted him with pseudo concern. 'I believe the latest model of this car has an optional new alarm system that actually cries, "Help, I'm being stolen"...'

She managed to keep her face straight as Jake gave her a look that should have turned her to cinders.

'Very funny,' he told her savagely, reaching into the car to pick up his car phone, but Lucianna shook her head and told him gently,

'It won't work, Jake, not whilst the alarm's ringing; there's an automatic bar that means you can't...'

'Where's the handbook?' Jake growled, reaching towards the glove compartment, but once again Lucianna shook her head sorrowfully.

'That won't open, Jake, not—'

'Not whilst the alarm's ringing… I know,' he cut in tightly. Then he asked her grimly, 'What about the engine? I suppose that won't start either…?'

'I'm afraid not,' Lucianna agreed gently.

'All right. You stay here; there's a public call box round the corner. I'll go and ring the garage.'

'All right, but you'd better leave me with the keys,' she told him dutifully, and explained, 'If you don't someone might think that I've tried to break in…'

Silently Jake handed her the keys.

Lucianna waited until he was out of sight and then went into action. Just as well she *had* ignored his veto on her touching his precious car…

Humming to herself, she set to work. Ignoring the alarm and overriding the system to open the glove box and remove the owner's manual, whilst deftly unlocking the bonnet, within three minutes she had silenced the alarm and within another two located the fault, which, as far as she could see, was simply a matter of replacing a fuse. The alarms would have to be reset, of course, because she had overridden them, but she still felt very pleased with herself as she stood back and enjoyed the consequent silence of her handiwork, patting the car and telling her that she was a very clever girl.

'What the…?'

She smiled as she turned round in response to Jake's ominous voice, telling him calmly, 'It's stopped…'

Out of the corner of her eye she could see a car bearing the insignia of the garage which had supplied Jake with his car. As it came to a halt alongside them Lucianna stepped forward and told the mechanic when he climbed out, 'I've overridden the central nervous system and removed the electronic data coil, but I think the main problem lies with one of the fuses...'

'More than likely,' the mechanic agreed, giving her an initial appraising and then approving look as he lifted the bonnet and checked what she had done.

'It's a problem we're having with these cars, and something that wasn't discovered in the re-testing stage. We suspect it could be caused by changes in the air temperature, but we haven't enough evidence to make a firm decision on that yet...'

That was all the encouragement Lucianna needed; within seconds the pair of them were deep in conversation and it took Jake's grim, 'When the pair of you have finished...' to bring the young mechanic's enthusiastic praise of the manufacturer's latest electronic system to a faltering halt as he turned his attention back to Jake's car.

Ten minutes later, after the mechanic had gone and they were driving out of the car park, Jake turned to Lucianna and demanded coldly, 'All right, Lucianna, you've had your fun. When...?'

Lucianna didn't pretend not to understand what he meant.

'Er...the weekend you had to fly to Brussels. You asked David to drive you to the airport and then collect you when you got back because you didn't want to leave the car parked there because so many had been stolen; so whilst it was at the farm...'

'You ignored what I'd said and decided to start playing around with it... You do realise that it could have been your interfering that caused the fault in the first place.'

She watched his mouth harden as he swung the car out into the road. It felt good to know that there was one area at least where her knowledge was superior to Jake's, and even better to know that he knew it as well—knew it and didn't very much like it, if his thunderous silence was anything to go by.

Lucianna paused in the act of watering the plants she had lovingly rescued, freeing their poor constricted roots from the prison of the over-packed pots in which they had been planted, repotting them in a much more generously proportioned home.

They had repaid her love and care by flourishing despite all the taunting comments of her brother. Her father had been one of the old school of farmers, disdainful and impatient of anything grown for mere ornament and pleasure, and as a girl Lucianna had tended her small garden in secret, guiltily aware that her father would not have approved.

Now things were different, though, and even her brother had been impressed the previous summer when her planters and hanging baskets had not only attracted admiring comments from her customers and visitors, but had also won first prize at the local country fair.

On the other side of the yard her brother and sister-in-law were deep in conversation. Against all her own expectations Lucianna had quickly discovered that the books Jake had persuaded her to buy were giving her a fascinating new insight into other people's reactions and feelings, and now, a week after their purchase, she was discovering that she was becoming something of a people-watcher.

The way her brother was leaning over his wife, the way their bodies were touching, the way she was smiling up at him were all indicative of their love and intimacy, and as she watched them Lucianna felt a painful welling of loneliness and envy.

Why was it that the ability to be attractive to and appeal to a man seemed to come so easily to others but not to her? Surely it wasn't just a matter of looking docile and demure, of deliberately appealing to a man's vanity, to his need to boost his own ego, because if it was she had too much respect for herself ever to adopt that kind of artifice. But no, it couldn't be. She only had to think of how strong Janey could be and how determinedly she held her own against David whenever she felt the need.

Sexual chemistry was easy to recognise but hard to define, according to *The Art of Flirtation*, and without it...

Lucianna turned back to her plants, but this time as she nipped off the dead heads her fingers weren't quite as steady. The relationship she had with John might not be smouldering with sexuality and passion but there *was* more to a good relationship, a meaningful relationship, the kind of relationship she, Lucianna, wanted with a man, than mere sex...

She glanced at her watch. Jake was due back this evening. He had been away on business for the last few days but he had telephoned her from his hotel this morning, instructing her to present herself at the Hall this evening so that they could start work on the new phase of 'The Plan'.

Out of the corner of her eye she suddenly noticed the way her brother's hand had dropped to Janey's stomach.

It was no secret to Lucianna that her brother and Janey had been wanting to start a family for quite some time. Did that small possessive gesture she had just witnessed mean that she had now conceived?

Thoughtfully Lucianna watched the way her brother kept his arm around his wife's shoulders as they walked back to the house together. He was certainly being rather more physically protective and careful of her these days…or was it simply that *she* was more aware of the subtle messages of other people's body language which had hitherto been a closed book to her?

'Jake's still obviously not got around to taking you shopping yet' David teased, as Lucianna joined them in the kitchen tugging affectionately on her hair. 'I can't wait to see what he's got in mind for you. It will have to be black, of course—that way the oil stains won't show.'

'David…' Janey began to warn, but Lucianna shook her head and smiled.

'It's all right, Janey,' she told her. 'I know when I'm being wound up.'

Yes, she knew, but in the past she had always reacted with defensive anger to such teasing, she acknowledged. Overreacted, some might say, but since her eyes had been opened to the power and the potential of using her body language to work for her she had discovered that there were far more subtle ways of getting her arguments across than verbal arguing— and apparently, if the book on flirtation was to be believed, more ways of attracting a man's interest than by dressing provocatively.

In the privacy of her own bedroom she had already secretly been practising the small, telling gestures which were supposed to draw a man's attention…

CHAPTER FIVE

HALFWAY through cross-questioning her on how much time and attention she had given the books she had bought, Jake had had to excuse himself to take a business call in the library. From the way he had been speaking to her since her arrival at the Hall she might have been a schoolgirl, Lucianna decided wrathfully, absently glancing at the TV screen she had just switched on, her eyes widening as she saw the couple on the screen start to kiss one another with passionate intensity. As the camera closed up on their faces Lucianna tensed and watched closely.

When she and John kissed she felt none of the intense passion this couple were so enviably sharing. No, John had certainly never kissed her the way the man on the screen was kissing the woman, holding her face in his hands as he pressed hungry, biting kisses onto her mouth and she responded, twisting and turning in his arms as though she couldn't get close enough to him.

Lucianna felt her heart start to beat faster, oblivious to Jake's return as she stared in fascination at the screen. The couple were kissing differently now, their mouths fused together, their breathing laboured.

'What's wrong, Lucianna? Hasn't John ever kissed you like that?'

At the sound of Jake's voice Lucianna spun round, her face burning hotly, embarrassed at being caught studying the screen as though she had actually been guilty of voyeurism.

'Y-yes, of course he has,' she told Jake fiercely, starting to stammer slightly and somehow unable to meet his eyes.

'I don't believe you,' she heard him challenge her suavely. 'In fact I don't believe you even know how to kiss like that...'

'Of course I do,' Lucianna asserted quickly.

'Yes? Then prove it,' Jake demanded softly. 'Come over here now and prove it to me, Lucianna... Kiss *me*...'

At first Lucianna thought that Jake couldn't possibly mean what he had said—either that or she must have misheard him—but when she searched his face for confirmation she realised with a fierce, sharp thrill of fear that he *had* meant it.

'You can't, can you?' she heard him saying softly to her. 'You can't and you don't—'

'I can,' Lucianna lied immediately.

'Prove it, then...'

How had Jake managed to move so quickly that he was now standing right next to her, one hand already cupping the back of her head, constraining her, preventing her from moving? His mouth was only centimetres away from hers. Nervously she licked her lips and heard him say, 'Well, that's an interesting start, but *you're* supposed to be the one kissing *me*, not enticing me into kissing you...'

Enticing him! Fear and anger, always a dangerously volatile cocktail of emotions, exploded inside her and before she could lose her courage Lucianna closed the distance between them, her lips firmly pressed together as she brushed them against Jake's mouth.

His lips felt cool and smooth and nothing whatsoever like John's, which if she was honest always felt just a little too wet and soft and—

'Call that a kiss? If *that's* the best you can do then no wonder you're having so much trouble with your love life... The wonder is that you've got one at all,' Jake told her succinctly.

Furious now, Lucianna opened her mouth to retaliate and then discovered that it was impossible for her to speak for the very good reason that, despite the fact that she was sure she *had* removed her lips from his, Jake's mouth was now covering hers, covering it and...

Involuntarily Lucianna's eyes widened, her gaze focusing helplessly on Jake's as she recognised that the movement of his mouth against her own felt nothing like John's and, moreover, that her response to it, to *him*, was nothing like anything she had ever experienced in her life before.

Why was her pulse hammering, over-revving so much that her heart felt as though it was going to jump into her throat? Why were her own lips trembling so much? Why did she feel this sudden strange, strong need to get even closer to Jake, so much so that she was, she recognised dizzily, actually pressing her body against his?

Why did she have this urge to make those soft keening, whimpering little sounds she could feel bubbling desperately in her throat?

'Jake...'

To try to protest had been a mistake, she realised seconds later as her lips parted but no sound emerged, for instead of being free to speak, it was Jake who had the freedom to cover her now open mouth with his and to keep it open by pressing his thumb against her chin whilst he slowly stroked the tip of his tongue back and forth against her parted lips.

It must be that the deliberately slow-building rhythm of what he was doing was having some sort of mesmeric effect on her, she decided in shocked bemusement, because instead of trying to stop him she was actually, she was actually…

A vision flashed behind her closed eyelids, a mental image of the couple she had been watching on the television screen and the way they had been kissing.

To her shock, almost as though he had been reading her mind, Jake started to kiss her in the same way—quick, biting kisses interspersed with softer, longer ones that for some reason compelled her mouth to cling helplessly to his.

She felt as though she was lost, adrift, drowning in the unfamiliar torrent of sensation that engulfed her. Beneath her clothes her body was behaving, reacting to Jake in a way it had never reacted to John, nor to anyone else. Jake was caressing the nape of her neck as he kissed her now and his tongue was beginning to make slow, sensual forays into her mouth.

His tongue!

Dizzily Lucianna dug her fingernails into Jake's arms, somehow managing to find the strength to tear her mouth away from his.

'You shouldn't have done that,' she told him stormily, all too conscious of her heightened colour and ragged breathing.

'No,' Jake conceded grimly. 'I shouldn't!'

Jake admitting that *he* was in the wrong? Lucianna could hardly believe it, and neither could she believe the extraordinary way in which she had responded to his kiss. In fact she wasn't going to believe it, she told herself hastily. She was going to forget that the whole incident had ever happened.

She darted a wary look at Jake who had gone to stand in front of the window. He had his back to her.

'Tomorrow afternoon we're going shopping,' he announced abruptly, startling her. 'And this time...' He paused and then told her, 'If you want to be treated like a woman, Lucianna, then you're going to have to learn to dress like one.'

Lucianna was far too relieved that he hadn't made any reference to what had just happened between them to object to his plans for a shopping trip, or to the comment which had accompanied his announcement of them.

And besides, one totally unexpected offshoot from the hours she had stubbornly forced herself to spend people-watching had been a tentative awareness that there *were* other modes of dress for her sex apart from the two completely opposing sides she had previously believed existed.

There had been that woman she had noticed the other day, for instance, wearing neatly pressed, well-fitting jeans, an immaculate white shirt and a cara-melly-coloured blazer which Lucianna had just known would feel wondrously soft to the touch, and to her own astonishment, as she'd studied her, Lucianna had experienced a wistful curiosity to know what it would be like to wear such clothes herself and with such confidence.

She had seen other women, of course, wearing garments she would never wear in a million years—tight, short Lycra skirts and equally tight, close-fitting leggings—but they too had exhibited the same careless confidence, a sort of insouciant ease which Lucianna was becoming increasingly aware that she did not possess.

She wore the clothes she did not just for practicality, as she had always insisted, she had been forced to recognise, but as a means of concealing herself, *protecting* herself. Almost as though if she was going to be accused of being unfeminine, unwomanly, then she might as well dress as though she wanted to be judged in that way.

She still wasn't sure where it had come from—this unfamiliar shy yearning for something different, to be someone different—and she was still very nervous and wary of it. But for the first time since she had started to grow up she was aware of a need within her to reach out towards the femininity she had previously fought so hard to deny.

Two hours later, with Jake still questioning her on her reading of the books she had bought, she had all but forgotten the turbulent and passionate moments she had spent in his arms.

Relaying the information she had gathered from the books back to Jake, she'd been surprised to discover just how much she *had* learnt, but if Jake was equally impressed he was concealing it well, his expression impassive, his profile turned slightly away from her, his whole manner towards her rather remote and withdrawn.

Only when she had impishly given him a demonstration of the 'mirroring' technique she had just been reading about did he actually seem to focus on her, but if the brief flash of anger she saw in his eyes was anything to go by he wasn't as surprised by her progress as she had expected.

'Jake...' Instinctively she reached out to touch his arm, unaware herself of just how much her quick mind had picked up from her reading or just how much her new knowledge was already reflected in the way she moved, talked and smiled. Ten days ago she would never have dreamed of touching Jake or any other man—but more especially Jake—to get his attention, and yet now she was doing it as naturally as though it were something she had always done.

She smiled teasingly at him as she said, 'I think perhaps *you* ought to read the books as well. You're supposed to respond to this...' she touched him lightly again and moved slightly closer to him, giving him another teasing smile '...by looking properly at me and moving closer to me.'

'It's John you need to practise your flirting techniques on, not me,' Jake told her harshly, moving away from her. 'I think we'd better call it a night...'

Half an hour later, as she drove home, Lucianna felt an odd sense of let-down and disappointment. What had she been expecting? she derided herself. Not praise from Jake, surely? She knew him far too well for that. For as long as she could remember and certainly since she had been a teenager, he had done nothing but criticise her.

Once Lucianna had gone, Jake poured himself a large glass of whisky. He wasn't normally a drinker, but right now...

Just what the hell had he got himself into? And why? He shook his head in self-resignation. He didn't really need to ask himself *that* question, did he? But until tonight he had managed to convince himself that his motives were, if not a hundred per cent altruistic, then at least ninety-nine per cent so.

Of course, what had happened tonight had blown that self-delusion totally apart. It had all been very well reminding himself at the start of how, as he had watched Lucianna growing up, he had often had to bite hard on his tongue to stop himself from quarrelling with her brothers, his friends, about the way they were treating their younger sister. Not that any of them had meant to hurt or harm her—it was just that because of their own upbringing they were unaware of how they were inhibiting her development as a woman, confident and happy in her femininity and her sexuality. He had seen…known, but then for him it was different. For a start, he *wasn't* Lucianna's brother.

Swearing under his breath, he poured himself another drink, going to sit down in one of the chairs drawn up close to the fire, resting his head back and closing his eyes.

He could still vividly remember the day, the hour, the moment he had recognised just how he really felt about his friends' baby sister, just why, when he was out on a date, instead of enjoying his date's company, he was constantly comparing her with Lucianna, knowing that he would rather be with her, enjoying her wickedly sharp sense of humour and its contrast with her still very naive emotions.

He had gone round to the farm to see David, the kitchen door had been open and he had walked in. The telephone, which was located in the kitchen, had started to ring. Upstairs he had heard a door open and then Lucianna had come running downstairs and into the kitchen, hastily wrapping a thin towelling robe around her wet and totally naked body as she did so.

As soon as she had seen him she had crimsoned with embarrassment, a floodtide of colour which had run up her body, scorching her tender, pale skin, filling her nipples with hot colour which had made them look...

Jake swallowed hard. There were some memories that haunted a man for all his life, some sins. She had been all of sixteen and he... He swallowed again. He doubted he would ever get over the sense of shock and self-disgust he had felt at the urge to take hold of her, to wrap her in his arms and plunder the tight virginity of those thrusting, colour-flushed nipples with the hot suckle of his mouth, until she twisted and arched against him, returning the white heat of passion that was coursing through him, scorching him, torturing him, possessing him with the same overwhelming fury with which he wanted to possess her.

Of course he had done no such thing. Of course he had forced himself to turn away whilst she turned and ran back upstairs, and of course neither of them had ever referred to the incident again. But from then on he had taken good care to distance himself from her both physically and emotionally...especially emotionally.

But, of course, it had been too little and far too late. He had been a man then, more than old enough to recognise what he was experiencing, even if that recognition had been coloured by his own distaste, his disgust with himself for falling in love with someone who was still only a girl...a child.

He had tried to cut himself off from what he was feeling, calling himself a pervert and worse, but none of it had done any good. He had, however, comforted himself that he was at least in control of his feelings, totally and absolutely... Until tonight...

And he still wasn't sure just what it had been about seeing her this evening that had destroyed the barriers he had painstakingly built to protect her. Certainly he hadn't enjoyed hearing her talking about John, and certainly the mental image he had had of her kissing him had stretched his self-control to its limits. But it had been more than that, he recognised. There had also been that new air she had about her, that subtle but oh, so alluring sudden awareness of herself as a woman, which he had returned to find her wearing like a little girl pirouetting proudly in her new dress.

How long would it be before she became even more self-aware, before she realised just *why* he was so determined to hold her at arm's length? And when she did—what then?

He glanced at the telephone. The temptation to ring the farm and say that their arrangement was off was almost overwhelming. It would be easy enough to invent some business trip that would keep him out of the way for a few weeks, but he already knew that he wouldn't do it, that he *couldn't* do it.

If he loved her as much as he claimed, then surely he loved her enough to help her get what she wanted, the *man* she wanted. And perhaps once she was safely engaged to him, married to him, he would finally be able to get on with his life.

Lucianna might not be a child any longer, but her feelings for him were still those she had had as a child. She still disliked and distrusted him and there was no way now that he could tell her just why he had had to make her feel like that towards him—no way, no point.

He closed his eyes again. Had she *any* idea just how close he had come this evening to totally losing control? Just how much he had wanted, ached for her?

'I thought Jake wasn't picking you up until two,' Janey commented with a smile as she caught Lucianna glancing through the kitchen window.

'He's not,' Lucianna agreed, flushing slightly.

'You know, if I didn't know better,' her sister-in-law teased, 'I'd think you were actually looking forward to this shopping trip.'

'Which just goes to show the sacrifices a woman is prepared to make to get her man,' David interjected, saving Lucianna from the need to defend herself and deny Janey's allegations.

They had told her this morning that, just as she had suspected, Janey was pregnant, and she had felt quite pleased to be able to say truthfully to them that she had half suspected as much.

'That sounds like Jake now,' Janey warned her as a car pulled into the yard. 'Looks like he's as eager for this shopping expedition as you are…!'

'Eager to get it over with,' David muttered. 'I hate shopping…'

'If that's the opening shot in a campaign of getting out of going to choose the nursery equipment, then it's one you're not going to win,' Janey told him cheerfully, laughing at his expression. 'And, unlike you, Jake enjoys shopping, and he's got excellent taste, unlike some men I could name.'

To Lucianna's surprise, once they were in the car Jake announced that he wasn't taking her into the local town but to a new shopping complex which had recently been opened several miles closer to the city.

Lucianna had heard about the complex via one of her customers, who had visited it to buy her outfit for her daughter's wedding. And, whereas the old Lucianna would immediately have objected that there was no point in him taking her there, since she had no intention of listening to his dictatorial views on what she should and shouldn't wear, this new Lucianna found that she was actually having to suppress a small bubble of female excitement as well as the sudden rush of apprehension and familiar dread that the thought of having to go into the—to her—unfamiliar and alien world of clothes normally gave her.

From her books she now understood that how a woman chose to present herself visually carried a very strong non-verbal message, and that the male sex was highly receptive and indeed vulnerable to visual messages.

And as for the impulse which had led her the other day to buy a couple of unbelievably expensive and glossy fashion magazines along with her newspaper and the new car magazine she had originally intended to buy, well, she'd told herself that if she had to endure the self-inflicted torture of having Jake boss her around and tell her what to do she might as well grab what extra help she could to make sure she kept her ordeal as short-lived as possible.

Once she had got over the shock at their cost and past her initial reluctance to turn the first page, she had discovered the cut and line of expensive clothes was, in many ways, as interesting to study as the design of a new car, and she had quickly found that, as with cars, her taste ran to the clean and simple, which would endure, rather than the fussy and over-ornamented—styles which were gimmicky.

And already, although Lucianna herself wasn't aware of it, what she had seen not just in the magazines but also through her people-watching exercises had begun subtly to exert an influence over her.

Jake, though, had noticed that the jeans she was wearing were a slightly better fit than the oversized ones she normally favoured, and the crisp white shirt, although still a man's and, he suspected, one she had purloined from her brother's wardrobe, was much more flattering than the heavy checked work shirts she normally wore.

Lucianna was forced to admit to herself that she was impressed by the shopping complex as she and Jake walked across the thankfully not too busy paved piazza area. Sapling trees, shrubs and attractive planters interspersed with seats, along with a good mixture of restaurants, bars and coffee shops, all of which had pleasant outdoor seating areas, all helped to lend a relaxing and almost continental atmosphere to the place, and Lucianna was also impressed by the absence of litter and general air of cleanliness.

'Where do you want to start?' Jake asked her. 'Or would you prefer to have a cup of coffee first?'

The thought of a cup of coffee was tempting, and not just as a means of a delaying tactic, Lucianna acknowledged, but she still shook her head determinedly.

Now that they were here she wanted to get the whole thing over and done with as quickly as possible.

'What's wrong?' Jake taunted her softly. 'Afraid you might lose your nerve?'

Lucianna flashed him a disdainful look and tossed her head, denying fiercely, 'Certainly not.'

Hiding his smile at her predictable reaction, Jake indicated a shop on the other side of the square.

Lucianna started to walk towards it and then stopped, frowning slightly and hesitating.

The understated elegance of the window display seemed to indicate that it would be one of those shops with the kind of assistants who would look down their elegant noses at her and make her wish she were a million miles away, but Jake was walking determinedly towards it and she wasn't going to have him thinking that she was nervous or, even worse, afraid.

'This shop is part of a European chain that specialises in providing a specific look which continues from season to season,' Jake explained.

'Really? How interesting,' Lucianna replied, covering her growing feeling of insecurity and panic with the sarcastic retort, adding, 'Well, that must make things easy for you, I suppose. If you bring all your girlfriends here for their clothes, then at least you won't miss recognising the latest one in the street.'

'And just what the hell is that supposed to mean?'

Lucianna was shocked into instant immobility as, instead of treating her comment with the contemptuous amusement she was used to, Jake suddenly wheeled round to confront her, his mouth a dangerously thin line and his eyes cold with anger.

'It…it wasn't meant to mean anything,' Lucianna denied. 'It…it was just supposed to be a…joke…'

'A joke?' Jake's eyebrows rose. 'Really? Well, I don't find it particularly funny to be accused of being the kind of man who has a chain of interchangeable bimbos dragging through his life, and for your information I have never suggested nor would I ever insult anyone by doing so, that a woman is some kind of doll, a toy, to be dressed up or undressed at my or any other man's whim. And furthermore I find it extremely unamusing, not to say offensive, that you should suggest I might,' Jake informed her acerbically.

Despite the fact that his obvious anger had shocked her, Lucianna fought back valiantly, determined not to be left wrong-footed, as she pointed out, 'Well, I'm sorry if I've got the wrong impression, but you're the one who's always changed his girlfriends more frequently than most men change their...their socks...'

'Really?' Jake challenged her. 'Do go on... It seems to me that you know more about my private life than I do myself.

'What a wonderfully insightful person you must be, Lucianna,' he marvelled sarcastically. 'And there I was thinking you never noticed anything that didn't come with wheels and an engine, and yet here you are, completely au fait with the most personal details of my life...more au fait than I am myself, as it happens, since the last time I had anything even approaching a relationship was—'

He stopped speaking as Lucianna, unable to control herself any longer, interrupted him hotly to say, 'I don't know why you're so angry, or pretending to be so...so... I heard the way David used to boast about the number of girls you and he took out,' she reminded him. Both her eyes and her voice mirrored her feelings, revealing to him far more than she knew as she added defensively, 'I thought it...you were...disgusting...boasting and bragging like that and—'

'Not me,' Jake interrupted her cuttingly. 'I don't recall ever having discussed such a subject in your hearing, and in fact...'

Forced by the sheer grim sternness of his voice to reconsider her own hotly, hastily spoken words, Lucianna was obliged to concede reluctantly, 'All right...I might never have heard you say it, but you were part of it...part of what David was talking about. You and he—'

'He and I might once have behaved with all the boorish stupidity that teenage boys are capable of displaying at times,' Jake interrupted her to agree, 'but the wholesale seduction and abandonment of a series of defenceless, vulnerable teenage girls in the style you were implying was totally and completely fictitious.

'For one thing, you underrate the intelligence and sense of self-preservation of your own sex if you think otherwise, Lucianna...and, for another, teenage boys have a capacity for self-aggrandisement and exaggeration that knows no limits. It's a fault that most of us grew out of very quickly indeed, and the kind of boastful comments teenage boys make shouldn't be taken too seriously, you know...'

Lucianna shivered slightly as she turned away from him, her voice low and slightly shaky as she told him passionately, 'I hated hearing the way you talked about...about girls...and...'

'Sex?' Jake supplied softly for her.

Lucianna could feel her face starting to burn. Why, oh, why had she ever brought up this subject? It was something she found it hard enough to think about herself even in the privacy of her own thoughts, never mind discuss with anyone else—and most especially with Jake.

'Yes, I can understand how some of the things you overheard must have made you feel.'

Pensively Jake watched her. Suddenly an awful lot of things were beginning to fall into place.

'No, you can't,' Lucianna contradicted him wildly, the panic starting to flood through her as she mentally relived the emotions and fears she had suffered through inadvertently listening in on her brothers' macho conversations coupled with the well-intentioned but clumsy lectures they had given her on the wisdom of the way she should behave with boys and the pitfalls that lay in wait for her if she didn't take heed of their advice.

'You're a man and you don't...you can't—' Abruptly Lucianna stopped, conscious that she had been on the verge of saying too much.

Jake, though, was refusing to let the subject drop, prompting gently, 'I can't what?'

Tight-lipped, Lucianna shook her head and looked longingly towards the interior of the shop. What ten minutes ago had seemed an inhospitable, unfriendly, alien place now seemed like a welcome haven when placed alongside Jake's unwanted probings into her most closely guarded thoughts and feelings.

'I can't *what*, Lucianna?' Jake persisted. 'I can understand how destructive, how emotionally and physically blighting it must be for a young girl on the brink of exploring her own sexuality and emotions to overhear a group of young men discussing such subjects without the guards they would normally put on their tongues in the presence of her sex.'

'It didn't do me any harm.' Lucianna immediately defended her brothers. 'In fact, it did me a favour. At least I knew what boys thought…'

'You knew what *boys* thought, yes,' Jake agreed quietly, 'but what about men, Lucianna? Did you…do you know how *they* think and feel, or did the lessons you inadvertently learned from your brothers go so deep that they instilled in you a fear and dread of being talked about as your brothers talked about their first sexual experiences? Did their conversations inspire in you such a dread of having all your dreams violated by the crassness of some boy who might later boast about his sexual conquest of you to his friends that sex is still something you view with distaste and embarrassment?'

'Of course not,' Lucianna denied quickly. 'In fact…' she tilted her chin towards him bravely as she lied '…I don't think anything of the kind… I—actually, I like sex; I like it a lot…'

'I see. So if I were to suggest that instead of continuing with our shopping trip you and I go back to the Hall and spend the afternoon in bed mutually enjoying sex you'd be perfectly happy to agree?'

Lucianna was almost unable to believe her ears, her shock showing in her eyes, her voice quavering betrayingly as she responded, 'No… No, I wouldn't.'

'But you just said you like sex,' Jake pointed out reasonably, 'and since I haven't had a relationship with anyone for quite some considerable time, and of course being a man…'

'I can't go to bed with *you*,' Lucianna protested squeakily.

'Why not? I'm no different from any other man,' Jake told her, adding silkily, with a deliberately sexual downward glance at her body, 'I don't intend to boast, but I think you'll find I'm equally satisfactory as any of the other men you've had.'

'Other men!' Lucianna's eyes rounded. 'I don't… there haven't… I think you're forgetting about John,' she managed to say.

'Ah, yes, John,' Jake agreed, but then added swiftly, 'But he isn't here, is he, and you and I…?'

Lucianna had had enough. Now that she was over the initial shock of Jake's astounding proposition, common sense was pointing out several salient facts to her. Tossing her head, she told Jake forthrightly, 'You're just trying to make fun of me. I know perfectly well you don't want to go to bed with me, you don't want to have sex with me…'

'You're right, I don't,' Jake agreed, but as he watched the emotions chase one another across her face he added mentally to himself, But I sure as hell want to make love to you, again and again and again, and if I had your precious brothers here with me now, friendship or not, I'd wring their wretched necks.

To Lucianna's relief he started to walk towards the shop, but as she made to follow him he stopped and turned back to her, catching her totally off guard as he asked her almost absently, 'Presumably there aren't any problems with the sexual side of your relationship with John…?'

Immediately Lucianna bridled.

'Of course there aren't,' she denied, thankful that Jake wasn't standing close enough to hear the way her heart was hammering. The last thing she wanted was for Jake of all people to discover her most closely guarded and shameful secret… which was that she was still a virgin.

Technically she knew what sex was all about, of course. How could she not do so with her outspoken elder brothers? Elder brothers who had not been merely outspoken in their frank teenage discussions about their own sex lives, when they thought she wouldn't understand or hear what they were saying, but who had been equally outspoken and frank in their fraternal advice to her about the way in which she should respond to any sexual approaches to herself.

'Say no and make sure you keep on saying no,' had been David's stern advice. 'That way they'll know they can't take advantage of you and they'll respect you.'

'Yes, and if they don't they'll have us to answer to,' Lewis had added fiercely.

What they *hadn't* told her, though, Lucianna recognised, was when and how a girl changed her no to a yes and, even more importantly, as she was discovering via her relationship with John, how she should let a man know that she was ready to be given the option to do so.

In the early days of their relationship John had certainly been keen enough to try and coax her into bed, and she, faithful to her brothers' stern lectures, had very firmly said no, but in the weeks before his departure he had seemed quite happy with the tepid kisses and caresses they had exchanged and Lucianna had been at a loss to know how to generate a little more passion between them.

When she had tried tentatively to snuggle up a little closer to him he had simply asked her if she was cold; when she had tried to deepen the kisses they had shared he had seemed oblivious to the hints she was trying to give him.

Hopefully, though, the tips she had picked up via the books she had bought should help her to make things clear to him, but it was a subject she certainly wasn't about to discuss with Jake. Jake, who, despite his surprising announcement earlier about the lack of any current relationship in his life, certainly had far more experience of her sex than she was ever likely to have of his.

Caught up in her thoughts, Lucianna suddenly realised that she had actually entered the shop and that the girl approaching her, far from being the haughty, disdainful type of person she had been dreading, was actually smiling at her with genuine warmth.

'Would you like some help?' she asked Lucianna. 'Or would you prefer to be left alone to browse?'

'We need—'

'I prefer to browse.'

Lucianna overrode Jake firmly, and just as firmly ignored his sardonic comment, meant for her ears only. 'This isn't a jeans shop, you know,' he said as the girl retreated, returning to the pile of jumpers she had been folding when they'd walked in, leaving Lucianna and Jake on their own.

'I *do* know that,' Lucianna returned with pointed emphasis, before turning on her heel and, ignoring Jake, walking over to study a selection of colour co-ordinated clothes which had caught her eye.

At first sight, the plain, caramelly-coloured co-ordinates for which she was heading might have seemed dull in comparison to the much brighter range of clothes the shop also carried, but Lucianna had remembered seeing similarly coloured clothes being modelled by a girl with her colouring in one of her fashion magazines.

She reached out and touched the fabric of a pair of trousers uncertainly. It felt cool and silky soft. She frowned as she studied the swing ticket. 'Tencel', it said, which left her none the wiser apart from her instinctive awareness that Tencel, whatever it was, made the fabric feel good and hang well.

There was a brochure on a coffee table beside her turned open at a page depicting the trousers she was currently examining. In the photograph they were teamed with a neatly fitting short jacket casually un-buttoned over what looked like a plain cream silk top.

'This is our newest range,' the salesgirl announced helpfully, suddenly materialising at Lucianna's side. 'It's my favourite and I've really fallen for the shell,' she added enthusiastically, whilst Lucianna looked blank and wondered frantically what on earth 'the shell' was until she saw that Jake had removed a hanger with the cream silk top on it and was holding it out to her.

He said quietly, 'Yes, it would suit you, Luce.'

The top, of course; she remembered now seeing it described as a 'shell' in her magazine. For once she was too grateful for Jake's intervention to object to his interference, but that still didn't quite explain, as she told herself later, quite just how she came to be standing in front of him half an hour later, self-consciously wearing not just the shell but the trousers and the jacket that went with it as well, along with the toning scarf, whilst the salesgirl enthused about the practicality of adding the sleeveless dress that was also part of the collection to the trousers, since the same jacket could be worn over it.

'I don't want...' Lucianna began, and then stopped,

a fiery blush staining her skin as she saw the way Jake was looking at her.

'What is it? What's wrong? Why are you looking at me like that?' she hissed defensively at him whilst the salesgirl went to find the dress.

Jake shook his head.

'Nothing's wrong,' he responded shortly, but he was frowning, Lucianna noticed, and suddenly the burning feeling of self-confidence and heady, unfamiliar pleasure in her own appearance that she had experienced when she had studied her reflection in the changing-room mirrors evaporated, bringing her abruptly back down to earth, making her feel awkward and uncomfortable and longing for the protection of her heavy denims to replace the silk trousers she was wearing.

As he turned his back on her Jake questioned with quiet inner savagery if he was totally sane. Knowing what he did about his feelings for her, it had surely been total madness to bring Lucianna somewhere where he was forced to watch her outer transformation from chrysalis to butterfly. He knew just what effect she was going to have on the rest of his sex when they saw her lovely lissom body dressed in that outfit, was aware that, whilst outwardly perfectly respectable, she seemed to hint with every movement she made at the delicate femininity of the body the suit was supposed to cover and shield.

'You really do have the most wonderful figure,' the salesgirl enthused, coming back with the dress over her arm and pausing to admire the effect of her coaxing and tweaking as Lucianna paused, reluctant to respond, to listen to her.

'And that colour is definitely you as well,' she

added truthfully. 'There's something about clothes like these that makes you feel and look so feminine, isn't there?' she said warmly, and Lucianna, who, after witnessing Jake's reaction, had been on the point of rejecting the outfit, hesitated and then frowned as she glanced into a mirror set at an angle to the shop floor several feet away.

In it she could just glimpse the back view of a woman wearing the same outfit as she was herself but on this woman it looked truly elegant, truly feminine. Lucianna lifted her hand to remove the scarf and then stood staring at the woman in the mirror, immobilised by the shock of realising that the reflection she could see was her own, that *she* was the woman who looked truly elegant, that the unfamiliar back view she had been admiring was, in actual fact, her own.

'I'll take it,' she told the girl positively, before she could allow herself to change her mind. 'All of it…and the dress as well,' she added.

The girl's smile widened.

Ten minutes later, as she paid for her purchases, Lucianna shot Jake a triumphant look.

He might not think she had what it took to be able to wear such feminine clothes but the salesgirl had thought differently and so had she, Lucianna decided firmly. She couldn't wait to see John's face when he saw her wearing her new things.

'I hope you don't mind my saying so,' the salesgirl commented to Lucianna as she handed her a huge carrier bag containing her new clothes, 'but I love the highlights you've had woven into your hair. Would you mind telling me where you had them done…?'

Highlights! Lucianna gave her a puzzled look, whilst Jake, who had overheard their conversation, duly explained for her, 'I'm afraid they're the work of the sun.'

'You mean they're natural? Lucky you,' the girl told her enviously. 'I have to pay a fortune for mine and they don't look anything like as good.'

Lucianna was still frowning as they left the shop. Highlights... Did the salesgirl mean those odd little goldy bits that had always lightened her hair in the summer?

'Coffee?' Jake suggested as he and Lucianna left the shop, but Lucianna shook her head and demanded instead,

'You didn't like it, did you? The outfit I just bought—you didn't like it. I could see it in your face...'

'On the contrary,' Jake assured her truthfully, 'I like it very much.' Where did it come from, he wondered ruefully, this female ability to sense and home in on any unwary male reaction with all the deadly accuracy of a heat-seeking missile?

'But you didn't like it on me,' Lucianna persisted. 'I suppose you think *I'm* not feminine enough, not *womanly* enough to wear it...'

Jake was frowning again now, she observed, his mouth hardening in that dangerous way that always made her heart start to beat just a little bit too quickly. Not that she was afraid of Jake's disapproval—no way...no way at all, she assured herself hastily.

'Anyway, I don't care what you think; it doesn't matter,' Lucianna informed him with a shake of her head before he could reply. 'It's what John thinks that matters...'

'What he *thinks* or what he *does*?' Jake demanded harshly, his own emotions overwhelming the need for caution and good sense. 'What kind of reaction is it you're expecting from him, Luce? What is it you want him to do? Take one look at you and want you so much that he can't wait to start ripping the things off you? Do you expect him to take one look at you and immediately declare his undying love? Because if you do...'

'Because if I do, what?' Lucianna challenged him angrily, her fingers curling tightly over the handle of the carrier bag as her face flushed with mortification. 'Just because *you* don't think I'm...that John loves me. Well, he does love me,' she told him proudly, 'and when he comes back...'

She paused, and Jake could see the tears she was fighting to blink away glittering in her eyes as he cursed himself inwardly for his stupidity. The last thing he'd wanted to do was to hurt her and he ached to be able to make her understand that loving someone, really loving them, had nothing to do with what they wore or how the rest of the world perceived them, and everything to do with what they were, and that a man who could only love a woman he could display on his arm like a pretty trinket wasn't, in his opinion, much of a man at all. But how could he?

CHAPTER SIX

'THIS way; we haven't finished yet.'

Lucianna frowned as Jake took hold of her upper arm in a firm grip and turned her towards the shop facing them.

'New underwear,' he added succinctly, although no explanation had really been needed—not with Lucianna well able to see what kind of apparel the shop he was indicating sold from the items on display in its window—undies which bore absolutely no resemblance whatsoever to the plain, sensible chainstore things she normally wore.

'I don't need any new underwear,' Lucianna denied untruthfully, glowering at Jake as she saw his disbelieving expression.

'No?' he questioned sardonically. 'You surely weren't planning to wear those no doubt sensible but far from sensually appealing items of female apparel you were removing from the washing line when I called round the other week for the welcome-home seduction scene you're planning for John's return, are you? Because if so...' He paused without finishing what he was saying, and added obliquely, 'Besides, they'd show through under those silky trousers.'

Lucianna opened her mouth to argue with him and then closed it again.

She *might* need new underwear to complement her new clothes but there was no way she was going to buy it with Jake there.

'I haven't got time today,' she told him loftily. 'I've got a customer's car booked in for a service at half past four.'

'Really? Well, in that case we'd better make a move,' Jake accepted. 'It's almost four now,' he told her.

They were halfway back to the car when he suddenly said musingly, 'I suppose you could always do without any underwear at all; that way the fabric would certainly hang well and of course, as you'll no doubt have learned by now from your books, from a man's point of view it's a very definite ego boost to know that a woman wants you so much that she's already prepared herself for sex with you and she wants you to know it.'

Lucianna stopped dead and gave Jake a murderous look, her face burning with angry heat as she denied furiously, 'I would *never* do anything like that... How dare you suggest I might?'

The naivety of her angry indignation should have made him feel guilty instead of pleased, Jake acknowledged as they walked on with Lucianna maintaining a stormy silence, because he recognised that he had deliberately used a verbal description to conjure up an image he'd known she would find unappealing.

He could have, for instance, told her that there was nothing a man, and more specifically himself, would have found more erotic and emotional, as well as physically arousing than the knowledge that the only tantalising barrier between his hands, his mouth and her skin was the outward formality of her elegant trousers and top, and that beneath them her skin, her body, was deliciously and wantonly naked. He could have told her that nothing was guaranteed to make him ache more than to be with her in a public place knowing that...

Determinedly he shook his head, reminding himself sternly of the danger of such thoughts.

It had been a shock to see her emerging from that changing room looking both so soignée and glamorous and yet at the same time too vulnerably unsure of herself. He had been hard put to it not to snatch her up into his arms and keep her there, to tell her exactly how he felt about her, how he had always felt about her, and for a moment the temptation had been such that it had been touch and go whether he would be able to control it—and himself.

Broodingly he watched her as she stormed across the car park ahead of him, still obviously angry with him, her head held high, shoulders back. Half of him wanted to take hold of her and show her physically if necessary just why a man who really cared, really loved her, would love her, want her exactly the way she was, and the other half prayed that she would never, ever have to suffer the disillusionment and pain of discovering just how unworthy of her love precious John actually was.

Lucianna hummed softly to herself as she gave the ancient Morris Traveller she had just been servicing a little pat.

Bessie belonged to one of their neighbours, Shelagh Morrison, and Shelagh herself had inherited the car from her grandmother in Dublin, who had, in turn, been given her as a gift by her late husband, Shelagh's grandfather, and Bessie was therefore considered to

be more of a family pet than a mere car and had to
be treated accordingly.

'She's horrendous to drive and expensive to keep
and, if I'm honest, I much prefer my BMW,' Shelagh
had confided once to Lucianna. 'And yet I just can't
bring myself to part with her. I'm just thankful that
you're able to service her for me. They told me at my
BMW dealership garage that I was lucky to have
found someone who could.'

Lucianna glanced at her watch now. She'd just got
time to get Bessie washed and polished before
Shelagh came to collect her. Her smile turned to a
small frown as she saw a car come racing down the
farm lane. Whoever was driving it was driving far too
fast for the lane and its country environment and
Lucianna's frown deepened as the car swung into the
yard and she recognised its driver.

What was Felicity doing out here? She hadn't come
to tell Lucianna that they'd had another fax from
John, presumably. Lucianna wiped her hands on her
dungarees and started to walk towards her.

In contrast to her own sensible mud- and farmyard-
proof dungarees and boots Felicity was wearing
spiky-heeled, strappy sandals and a short—very short,
Lucianna noticed—white dress.

'Oh, Luc, good! I'm glad you're here!' Felicity ex-
claimed as soon as Lucianna was within earshot. 'My
car is making the most peculiar noise; could you look
at it for me?'

'I can,' Lucianna agreed, glancing immediately at
the car's relatively new number plate, 'but isn't it still
under warranty?'

She remembered how impressed John had been
when Felicity's then boyfriend had bought her the car

as a twenty-first-birthday present, commenting much to Lucianna's chagrin, 'But you can't blame him for going overboard and trying to impress her. She *is* a real stunner...'

Stunner or not, she was certainly not mechanically minded, Lucianna decided ten minutes later, having run the engine of the Toyota and heard it making no noise other than a clean, healthy purr.

'What sort of noise was it making exactly?' she asked Felicity cautiously once she had checked out all the obvious potential faults.

'I don't really know...it was just...you know, a noise...' Felicity told her unhelpfully. 'Heavens, you are clever,' she added. 'I don't know the remotest thing about car engines. Not that I would particularly want to,' she added. 'All that dirt and grease... It must ruin your nails and your hands. Ugh...

'By the way,' she added conversationally when Lucianna made no response, 'who *was* that guy you were with when I saw you in town the other day? I rather thought I recognised him from somewhere but...'

'Jake, you mean?' Lucianna asked her as she closed the bonnet of the car. 'He's...' On the point of launching into an explanation of Jake's background and position in their local society, she suddenly changed her mind, alerted by some female sixth sense as to what was really behind Felicity's seemingly innocent question—which was confirmed by the predatory, eager look in the other girl's eyes. 'Oh, he's just a neighbour,' she said dismissively instead.

'A neighbour?' The other girl's eyes widened slightly and then narrowed as she gave Lucianna an assessing look before starting to smile and then laughing. 'That's typical of you, Luc,' she commented, and then added for no apparent reason, 'I could never do a job like yours.'

'So you've already mentioned,' Lucianna agreed tersely.

'I'd hate having to wear such unfeminine clothes,' she continued, apparently oblivious to Lucianna's increasing desire to bring her call to an end. 'I like to wear soft, silky things next to my skin—silk underwear... Do you ever wear silk underwear, Luc?'

'Not under my dungarees,' Lucianna returned woodenly.

'I don't suppose you ever wear stockings either, do you, Lucianna?' she queried, giving Lucianna a faintly malicious look. 'John often teases me about wearing them.'

Lucianna looked away from her, determined not to let her see how hurtful she found her revelations—revelations which she was beginning to suspect were fully intended to *be* hurtful and to underline the differences between them. Well, anyone could buy a pair of stockings—and wear them. Lucianna's heart suddenly seemed to start beating a little faster.

That was twice now within the same twenty-four hours that she had been told that her choice of underwear lacked man-appeal, and even the book she had been reading on flirtation had stressed that it was perfectly acceptable for a woman to indulge in a small amount of sensually teasing dressing.

She took a deep breath as she came to a sudden decision.

'I can't see that there's anything wrong with your car,' she told Felicity firmly. 'But it might be as well if you took it back to the dealership and got them to check it over just in case.'

She looked at her watch. 'I'm sorry but I've got to get the Traveller washed and polished before its owner comes back for it.' And then, quite deliberately, she turned away from the other girl to show her that she expected her to leave.

If Felicity was so determined to make fun of her then Lucianna couldn't stop her, but she certainly wasn't going to help her, nor was she going to let her use her as a means of trying to get an introduction to Jake.

Did she really think that she, Lucianna, was so stupid, so lacking in female awareness, that she wouldn't realise just what she was really after underneath all that patently untrue concern about her car? If Felicity had been a little bit more open and honest with her, if she hadn't taken such delight in underlining the fact that John found her attractive, then she might have felt more inclined to help, Lucianna decided. And she might even have felt enough female fellow-feeling for her to warn her that Jake was no stranger to female admiration, even though he might have said to *her* this afternoon that it had been a long time since his last relationship.

Determinedly keeping her face averted, Lucianna didn't turn round until she heard the Toyota's engine die away as the other girl drove back the way she had come.

If she was so interested in Jake then let her find another way of bringing herself to his attention. The two of them would be well suited, Lucianna decided angrily.

* * *

'What's wrong with you? You haven't spoken a word all through supper,' David said in concern.

'Nothing's wrong,' Lucianna told her brother quickly.

In point of fact the reason why she had not contributed very much to the suppertime conversation was that she was still reflecting on the events of the day. As she looked towards the window, she was mentally contrasting the visual difference between her own dungaree-clad body and the sultry, deliberately sensual swing of Felicity's hips in the short skirt she had been wearing, the way she had run her fingertips down along her thigh as she'd moved. She recalled the other girl's comment about how John teased her about her stockings.

There had been stockings in the window of that underwear shop Jake had directed her attention to this afternoon—stockings attached to the most frivolously feminine garter, with a tiny pair of briefs to match.

'I'm going over to Ryedales tomorrow. They're taking delivery of a new state-of-the-art harvester and bailer. Want to come with me?'

Lucianna looked at her brother then shook her head.

'I can't,' she told him. 'I've…I've got some shopping to do.'

Behind Lucianna's back Janey quickly and very firmly shook her head in her husband's direction, warning him not to make any comment.

'Lucianna going shopping… I don't believe it,' David commented to Janey later, when they were on their own. 'She's really got it badly for this John.'

'She's a *woman*, David,' Janey reminded him gently. 'And she's just beginning to discover the pleasure of what being a woman means, of taking pride in herself and her femininity.'

'But she's always been such a tomboy...'

'Because that was what all of you *expected* her to be,' Janey told him firmly. 'But she isn't a teenager any more, she's a woman now, and a very, very attractive one...'

'Luce?'

'Luce,' Janey confirmed, shaking her head in faint exasperation at the brotherly disbelief in his voice and adding spiritedly and, so far as David was concerned, very cryptically, 'And if you don't believe *me* then ask Jake...'

'Jake...? What...?'

Shaking her head again, Janey gave him an enigmatic smile.

Men. Why was it that even the nicest of them could be so obtuse at times?

'Jake's been on the phone,' Janey announced as Lucianna walked into the kitchen the following morning. 'He's got to go away for a few days—something about some business matters needing attention. He said to tell you that he'll be back by the end of the week.'

Jake was away. Lucianna's heart gave an unexpectedly intense flurry of small thuds which she told herself quickly were no doubt due to relief that she would be relieved of his odious and demanding presence for a small oasis of time.

She suddenly found herself wondering whether these business matters Jake so unexpectedly had to attend to might involve the presence of a female travelling companion, a someone with whom Jake might share whatever private time these business matters might allow him, a someone who might *enjoy* being taken shopping and dressed up in those same, so silky, frivolous bits of nonsense which had kept manifesting themselves throughout her troubled dreams last night.

Not that *she* cared. No, of course she didn't. Why should she? Jake could buy underwear for as many other females as he chose—it was nothing to her! Nothing at all.

Janey frowned as Lucianna pushed away her cereal virtually untouched. Perhaps David *was* right after all and Lucianna *did* genuinely love John. Janey sincerely hoped not—for several reasons!

'I'd better go upstairs and get changed. I've got some shopping to do this morning,' Lucianna told her sister-in-law, abruptly coming to the decision she had been tussling with.

It was an easy enough task for Lucianna to drive to the shopping complex and find the shop Jake had pointed out to her the previous day. What proved far harder was actually making herself open the shop door and go inside.

In the end it was the friendly and slightly concerned smile of the girl behind the counter inside the shop, who had already glanced in her direction several times, that finally gave Lucianna the impetus to push open the door and go in.

'It *is* hard to choose, isn't it?' the girl commented as Lucianna glanced uncertainly around, thoroughly bewildered not just by the multiplicity of styles and colours in which the underwear was displayed but also by the confusing language in which it was de-

scribed. 'Would you like some help?' the salesgirl
continued.

Lucianna took a deep breath, nodding. Since she
was the only customer in the shop she didn't exactly
feel comfortable fibbing that she was simply brows-
ing.

'Are you looking for something for yourself?' the
salesgirl queried, and when Lucianna nodded again
she enquired further, 'Is it for a special occasion or
to go under a specific outfit? For instance, we recommend either a string or these to go under trousers,'
she explained, taking in Lucianna's jeans-clad figure
with a brief but professional glance and pointing to a
nearby display.

The 'string', as she described it, made Lucianna
gnaw worriedly at her bottom lip. She could just
imagine Jake's reaction to the idea of *her* wearing
such a delicate feminine wisp of underwear.

'It's far more practical and hard-wearing than it
looks,' the salesgirl informed her, taking it off its
hanger and proving her point by stretching the skimpy
white lace garment.

'I wear them myself, and they're great under even
the tightest jeans or anything where you don't want
to show any knicker line. My boyfriend thinks they're
rather neat as well,' she added with a conspiratorial
grin.

'We do sell these as well, of course,' she added,
her voice and expression thoroughly professional once
more as she replaced the string with its fellows and
removed the other pair of knickers she had pointed
out to Lucianna.

'Big knickers, we call them,' she explained wryly,
'and of course they do give an equally neat outline,

but we do tend to find that they don't sell quite as
well as the strings. Men don't like them,' she told
Lucianna, before turning away and waving her hand
around the shop floor. 'Of course, if you're after
something a little bit more frivolous, something that's
more flirty than functional, we do several mix-and-
match ranges that include everything from silk or
satin teddies right through to balconette bras, French
knickers...'

Lucianna took another deep, steadying breath and,
before she could lose her nerve, blurted out,
'Er...actually, I was wondering... Do you sell suspender belts?'

To her relief the girl didn't betray by so much as
a flicker of an eyelash that she found anything unusual
in her request.

'Oh, yes, they're over here,' she told Lucianna, indicating and walking towards another display.

'I must say I don't wear them very often myself
since I tend to go for trousers rather than skirts, but
just once in a while I have to admit there's something
rather special and sexy about wearing stockings.

'This is one of our most popular ranges, especially
with brides,' she said, removing a delicate garter belt
of white silk and lace from the rack and holding it
out for Lucianna's inspection. 'We do a matching
strapless bustier-cum-corset piece, which is ideal for
strapless dresses, but if it's just the belt you want I
can definitely recommend this one. And these are the
briefs that go with it,' she added, reaching for a pair
which Lucianna could see on a display behind her.

'Of course, you'll probably need a small size,' she
added thoughtfully, subjecting Lucianna to a professional inspection. 'And if you were thinking of buying

a bra to go with them as well, then I'd definitely recommend that we measure you properly to make sure
we get the right fit.'

In the end it was a good two hours before Lucianna
finally left the shop.

In addition to the suspender belt and two pairs of
stockings she had also bought the briefs and a pretty
bra that matched the belt and briefs, although she had
complained to the salesgirl that there was so little of
it that she wasn't sure how on earth it could be so
expensive.

'Wait until the man in your life sees you wearing
it,' the salesgirl had advised her with a grin. 'Then
you'll know it was worth every penny! Trust me...I
know!'

She had also purchased two other bras in a shim-
mery and virtually transparent soft, coffee-coloured
Lycra, and their matching strings, which the girl had
assured her were just the thing to wear beneath white
or any kind of transparent fabric, since, once on, their
unusual colour meant that they could not be detected.

Once outside again in the sunshine, Lucianna decided that the odd and unfamiliar sense of light-
heartedness and recklessness that seemed to be pro-
pelling her across the piazza in the direction of a shoe
shop the salesgirl had recommended to her must have
something to do with the fact that she hadn't eaten
her breakfast—just like the disturbing mental images
that kept on popping up out of nowhere, showing herself dressed in all her new finery—including the new
underwear—whilst Jake gazed on in stunned awe!

Why on earth it should be Jake rather than John
who was stunned speechless by her transformation she
had no clear idea... Perhaps it had something to do

with the fact that it was Jake who had suggested she buy the stuff in the first place.

The saleswoman in the shoe shop showed every sign of being equally helpful and knowledgeable about the goods she was selling as the girl in the underwear shop had been, but by now Lucianna was well into her own stride and, with an aplomb and sense of assurance which startled herself a little, she very quickly and calmly picked out a pair of light-weight shoes to wear with her new silk suit plus a pair of strappy sandals which, as yet, she had nothing in her wardrobe to wear with—unless, of course, you counted the stockings and suspenders!

It was now definitely time for her to go home, Lucianna decided dizzily as she emerged from the shop clutching her parcels, but first she needed a cup of coffee. And it was whilst she was seated on the pavement under an umbrella to protect her from the heat of the sun that she noticed the banner hanging in the window of the chemist's on the other side of the road, announcing that they were giving free make-up demonstrations and make-overs to anyone who wished to avail themselves of this treat.

Without knowing quite how it had happened, Lucianna found herself inside the chemist's enjoying the cool draught of their air-conditioning whilst she studied the vast array of cosmetics on sale.

Her brothers had teased the life out of her when she had first started experimenting with make-up in her early teens, and David had even gone so far as to make her wash off the garish red lipstick and bright blue eyeshadow which she had secretly saved her pocket money for weeks to buy. But the kind of make-up on sale here was very different from the cheap, brightly coloured cosmetics she had bought as a young girl, she realised. Very different...

'Would you like some help?'

As she turned her head towards the smiling sales-girl approaching her, Lucianna bowed to the inevitable.

Back at the farmhouse David glanced frowningly at his watch.

'Luce can't *still* be shopping,' he told Janey. 'She's been gone for over *four* hours.'

'Of course she can,' Janey replied smugly, adding with a smile, 'She's a woman.'

Thoroughly baffled, David retreated into the farming article he had been reading. *He* might not be an expert on the female sex like Jake was, but he knew when he was beaten!

'It would be just your luck for this—' Janey patted her small bump lovingly '—to turn out to be a girl,' she told him, correctly guessing what he was thinking.

'Girl or boy, I don't honestly mind,' David told her truthfully, putting down his magazine and walking round the table to take her in his arms and hold her, hold them both, tenderly. 'In fact, so far as I'm concerned you can go ahead and produce a whole tribe of girls...'

'*I* can produce?' Janey scoffed. '*You're* the one who decides what sex our offspring are going to be, and as for us having a tribe...'

CHAPTER SEVEN

LUCIANNA frowned critically as she studied her reflection in her bedroom mirror. With David and Janey out of the way on a rare night out together, she had taken the opportunity to experiment with her new make-up purchases, and not just her make-up, she acknowledged as she stared intently into her mirror, trying to gauge if she had followed the salesgirl's advice, or if she ought to add just a touch more depth to the eyeshadow she had so carefully and nervously applied.

'With your colouring, taupes and muted colours will suit your eyes best,' the girl had told her, laughing sympathetically when Lucianna had relaxed enough to tell her ruefully about her unhappy experiments with bright blue eyeshadow.

Now, with the taupe eyeshadow highlighting the size and colour of her eyes, Lucianna was slightly startled to see how both that and the softly pretty coral lipstick she was wearing brought out and emphasised the femininity of her facial features in a way which made her look and feel very different from her normal workaday self.

Would John be similarly surprised?

He had rung her earlier in the day, but she had had a customer waiting to collect her car and so their conversation had been rushed and not very satisfactory. John had sounded distant and on edge, more concerned with telling her all about the way he was being fêted by his colleagues in the Canadian office than interested in talking to her about their own relationship.

Their relationship.

Rather nervously Lucianna stepped back from the mirror and studied her reflection full-length, forcing herself not to look away from what she saw but to examine herself. It was just as well she wasn't wearing any blusher—the rosy glow colouring her skin was more than colour enough—and even though she knew it was ridiculous to feel embarrassed by her own reflection, and in the privacy of her own bedroom, Lucianna couldn't help it. The reflection in front of her was just so very different from the one she was used to seeing.

After she had finished work she had showered and washed her hair, which was still hanging loosely around her shoulders in a thick, silky cloak which she privately deemed rather untidy but which for some reason seemed to highlight the delicacy of her facial bones and the softness of her skin. But it wasn't her face or her hair which was causing her to feel abashed. No, it was the fact that she had taken advantage of David and Janey's absence not just to try out her new make-up but to try on her new undies as well.

What would John think if…when he saw her like this…? Would *he* notice, as she had done herself, how delicate and slender her legs looked clad in such sheer stockings? Would he…? What would he think… say…Lucianna took a deep gulp of air…when he saw the frivolous lacy affair that was holding them up? What would his reaction be to her new bra—a bra which was nothing like any she had ever worn and which it had taken all the salesgirl's earnest professionalism and sincerity to assure her was perfectly respectable and one of their customers' firm favourites?

And, as if all that weren't enough, there was, of course, the string. Lucianna took another gulp of air… From the front it looked if not exactly as sturdy as her normal knickers then certainly not more revealing than a rather high-cut bikini, but from the back…! As yet she hadn't managed to pluck up the courage to study her back view, and the mirror in her room wasn't exactly ideal for doing so.

In Janey and David's room there was a much better full-length mirror which could be angled. Lucianna glanced doubtfully at the high-heeled sandals she was wearing. So far she had only walked across her own bedroom floor in them—and had felt as vulnerable and awkward as a newborn colt.

Taking a deep breath, she reminded herself that sooner or later she was going to have to appear in them in public, so the sooner she learned to walk properly in them the better, and since she could hardly service her customers' cars wearing them she had better make use of every chance she got to practise.

After all, there was no one around to witness her ineptitude, nor her shy awareness of how very different she looked and felt, nor how very much more aware of herself, her body, her womanliness, she suddenly was.

She started to walk tentatively towards the bedroom door.

The business meeting he had been called to in Paris so unexpectedly to attend had proved rather more fraught than Jake had anticipated but, in the end, he had had his way—but not before he had had to argue his point with some force. Along with the estate, he had inherited a considerable portfolio of stocks and shares to which he had, over the years, added other investments of his own, latterly moving into the area of helping others to set up their own small businesses and taking not just a financial but also a managerial interest in those businesses.

It was a high-risk enterprise and one which required steady nerves as well as a good deal of patience and faith in one's own judgement, and Jake's trust in his own judgement had been sorely tested of late.

There had been a delay at Charles de Gaulle and it had been a hot day; he was glad to be free of the stale, fume-filled air of the motorway but the drive home was not giving him its usual sense of release and pleasure. He turned off the main road and into the lane that led both to the farm and then on to his own home; he automatically checked his speed as he drove past the turn-off for the farm and then, instead of accelerating, for some reason he wasn't prepared to analyse, he braked instead.

Braked, stopped, reversed, and then finally took the side turning for the farm.

A little uncertainly at first, then with increasing confidence as she got used to the height of them, Lucianna walked up and down the landing in her new, delicate, high-heeled sandals. It certainly felt most peculiar, but not in the least unpleasantly so.

She frowned a little critically as she caught sight of her unvarnished toenails. The stockings she was wearing were completely sheer, designed to be worn, if necessary, with open-toed shoes, and it seemed now to Lucianna that a pretty but discreet application of a soft shiny colour to her toenails would complement both her shoes and the sheer delicacy of her stockings, rather in the same way that she would have advised a customer that those all-important touches such as keeping the bodywork of their cars clean and polished were also part and parcel of keeping their vehicles in good working order.

Now that she had mastered the art of walking in her new shoes—well, sort of—it was time to venture into David and Janey's room and study her reflection in their mirror.

Once she was inside their room, though, Lucianna found she was having great difficulty in bringing herself to look at what she was wearing. Her heart had started to beat very fast and she was conscious of a mixture of apprehension and nervous excitement churning in her stomach.

Unsteadily, she turned her head in the direction of the mirror and then tensed in shock. Was that really her? That unexpectedly tall, long-legged creature— long-legged woman? she corrected herself shakily. And those curves...that tiny waist, those softly rounded breasts; where had they come from? She didn't normally make a habit of studying her own naked body but surely she would have known, noticed, if her body was really as sensual, as womanly as its mirror image now reflected? Was it the soft light of David and Janey's bedroom that gave her skin its satiny sheen?

Hesitantly, Lucianna touched the smooth swell of her breast above the dainty cup of her bra and then flushed. She looked so different, so... Peeping over her shoulder, she glanced uncertainly at her neatly curved and very provocatively rounded rear.

Totally absorbed in what she was seeing, she didn't hear Jake drive into the yard and stop the engine of his car.

The lights were on in the farmhouse kitchen and upstairs as well and, out of habit, Jake merely knocked briefly on the unlocked kitchen door before pushing it open and walking in. After all, he had been a regular visitor here at the farmhouse from boyhood and had long ago been instructed by David and Janey that he was not to stand on ceremony, that so far as they were concerned he was virtually an adopted member of the family.

The fact that there wasn't anyone in the kitchen wasn't particularly unusual; it was too early in the evening for David and Janey to have gone to bed, and since he had noticed as he'd driven up that their bedroom lights were on he opened the kitchen door and stepped into the hall, intending to call up to warn them of his arrival, but, before he could do so, their bedroom door opened.

The uncertainty in Lucianna's movements as she opened David and Janey's bedroom door and stepped out onto the landing wasn't due as much to her unfamiliar footwear as to her unfamiliar self.

If the reflection of herself she had seen in the dress shop earlier in the week had surprised and pleased her that was nothing to the emotions she had experienced just now. Her reflection might have unnerved her somewhat but there was no doubting its femininity...its sexuality...*her* femininity and sexuality. She paused in the open doorway, arching her neck, standing proudly, a small, secret smile curling her mouth.

Let Jake try telling her now that she needed to look to others to learn how to be a woman; that she needed to adopt their body language in order to make John appreciate her.

Suddenly, and for the first time in her life, Lucianna knew how it felt to be proud of her womanhood, of her body, and it showed in the way she held herself and moved as she started to walk towards her own room.

And how it showed!

Initially, standing in the hallway below her, Jake simply couldn't believe his eyes—or rather his brain was having difficulty in accepting that what he saw, *who* he saw, was Lucianna. His body was experiencing no such problems. *It* had recognised her straight away, recognised her, known her, reacted to her and was still reacting to her, and suddenly all the emotions he had been fighting to control for what, right now, felt like more than half his lifetime, exploded in a self-igniting flash of feral anger that caused him to take the stairs two at a time, blocking off Lucianna's access to her bedroom with his body as he demanded furiously, 'Lucianna…what the hell do you think you're playing at?'

To say she was shocked didn't begin to go anywhere near describing Lucianna's feelings.

The totally unexpected sight of Jake coupled with the intensity of his anger would have been enough to put her on the defensive at the best of times, but to be confronted by it and by him in her present state of undress… It would have been bad enough to have been surprised by anyone, even to be faced by Janey, just at the moment. The only reason she had found the courage to do what she had just done, to try on her new underwear and… Well, the only reason she had done what she had was that she had been secure in the knowledge that she had the house completely to herself.

And if anyone had asked her who the last person, the very last person was whom she would have wanted to see her like this she would immediately have said Jake. And yet here he was, looking at her with such savagery, such fury that…

'Where is he?' she heard Jake demanding furiously as he reached out to constrain her, to grab hold of her wrist, preventing her from fleeing, retreating back into David and Janey's bedroom.

'He…? What he?' Lucianna queried in bewilderment as she tried to prise his fingers free of her wrist.

'What he? The one you've dressed yourself up like that for of course,' Jake told her bitingly. 'And don't tell me there is no "he", Lucianna, because I won't believe you.' His eyes scanned her body, causing her face to burn a hot, embarrassed dark pink and then her whole body to become scorched with the same colour. She suddenly realised that for some totally unfathomable reason her nipples beneath the delicate fabric of her new bra had hardened and were now quite clearly visible in all their pouting provocation, and Jake had seen them; that much was clear from the way he turned his head and looked so intently at her body.

Instinctively, she placed her free arm across her breasts, her eyes flashing daggers of embarrassed fury at him.

'It's a bit late for that,' Jake told her scathingly. 'You might as well be stark naked—you damn well nearly are.'

'I am *not*,' Lucianna denied. 'I'm wearing the new underwear *you* told me to buy,' she defended herself bravely.

'*I* told you to buy?' Jake checked himself and frowned. 'Don't try to tell me you bought this stuff you're wearing—this...these—because of me,' he told her bitingly.

'Why not?' Lucianna challenged him recklessly. 'It's the truth; you were the one—'

Abruptly she stopped speaking, her face going bright scarlet as she realised what she had been about to say, what she couldn't possibly say, and that was that five minutes ago, standing in front of her brother and sister-in-law's bedroom mirror, although it might have been John's reaction to her transformation and her shy realisation of her own sexuality she had first of all been thinking about, to her chagrin, it had been Jake's voice, Jake's face, Jake's reaction she had instinctively pictured.

Just for those few heart-stopping and instantly rejected heartbeats of time it had been Jake's hands, Jake's mouth, Jake's touch she had emotionally imagined caressing her near-naked body. To her horror, even as she fought back the treacherous memory of those few fatal seconds, her body was already wilfully reacting to it, her nipples flouting her fervent plea to them not to betray her, whilst deep down inside her body...

'So you dressed like this because of *me*?' she heard Jake demanding grittily and disbelievingly, releasing her wrist abruptly as he added with a growl, 'Lucianna...'

But as she turned in instinctive response to the harsh command in his voice suddenly his expression changed completely, his hand reaching out towards her again but not this time to restrain her in the old, familiar critical grip he had used on her since her childhood, but, far more dangerously, to gently cup the soft swell of her breast. His thumb caressed the naked flesh above the low-cut cup of her new bra, caressing it and, Lucianna recognised dizzily, edging the fabric even lower so that she could quite clearly see the flushed dusky pink flesh surrounding her nipple and, even more disturbing, feel the urgent pulse of her nipple itself, as though it were silently urging Jake to pull away the fabric altogether.

'*Because* of me?' she heard Jake repeating in a very different voice from the one he had used earlier, a voice which held an unfamiliar, faintly rusty but wholly male message of urgency and arousal. 'Or *for* me?'

For him…? Lucianna opened her mouth to deny any such thing, heard Jake say her name in an excitingly harsh voice she had most certainly never heard him use before, and automatically and instinctively took the small provocative step, the fatal step forward that closed the minute distance between them, her body swaying provocatively, unsteadily, as she tried to balance on her new shoes, throwing her forward against him.

'Oh, God,' she heard Jake mutter under his breath, 'I must be crazy doing this.'

Doing what? she tried to ask, but found she couldn't say a single thing, for the very simple reason that Jake's mouth was now covering hers and silencing every sound she tried to make, including her small shocked squeak of protest.

Later she would try to tell herself that it must have

been the new shoes that caused her to feel so dizzy, just as it must have been the fact that she was only wearing her underwear that made her shiver and draw closer to the warmth of Jake's fully clothed body— fully clothed maybe, but she was not so naive that she couldn't recognise the surging hardness of his body as she pressed her own against him and then pressed herself against him again, carried away by the novel discovery that what she had read in her books had quite patently been correct and that men were responsive to a woman's body language.

Lost in the heady awareness of the power of her sensuality, she was dimly aware of Jake groaning hoarsely as he cupped her face with both hands, but it was only when she felt the urgent thrust of his tongue within the vulnerable cavity of her own mouth that she recognised just what her innocent experimentation had done. By then...by then, inexplicably, all she really wanted to do, all she could actually *think* of doing, was to wrap her arms around Jake just as tightly as she could whilst her senses spun under the sensual assault of his kiss.

When he finally paused to lick the outline of her mouth with the tip of his tongue and command, 'Kiss me back,' it seemed to be the most natural, the most *essential* thing in the world to do just as he had asked, tentatively at first and then with more assurance as she discovered the heady delight of exploring the moist heat of his own mouth with the darting, uncertain tip of her tongue.

But it was when he captured it, held it prisoner and slowly, delicately sucked on it that she finally realised how out of her depth she was and in what dangerous waters—waters in which the only thing she had to cling to, in which her only safety and security lay in trusting herself completely to Jake and letting him take the responsibility for her.

She opened the heavy-lidded eyes she had closed, trembling in his arms as he traced her swollen mouth with his fingertip. He told her huskily, as she shuddered under the sensual caress, her mouth unbelievably sensitive to his touch, 'If that's how you react to being kissed, I can just imagine how you're going to feel when it's your breasts, your nipples—you—that I'm sucking and kissing…'

Lucianna couldn't help it; she felt the shock of his words rip right through her body in a convulsive surge of sensual need and surrender, and without even realising what she was doing she heard herself moaning his name whilst her hands went to her breasts—whether to conceal them or tear away the fabric that covered them, to show him just what effect his words were having on her, she didn't really know; but Jake, it seemed, did, and the cool rush of air that preceded the hard warmth of his hands holding her naked breasts as he pulled away her bra only seemed to increase the hot, spiralling ache pulsing through her whole body.

Jake was kissing the side of her neck whilst his hands caressed her breasts, his mouth, hot and hungry, scorching her naked skin, and yet instead of feeling shocked she actually seemed to be welcoming it, wanting it.

Lucianna heard herself moan again as her body ached against Jake's hands, the rough pads of his thumbs moving against her nipples sending her into a frenzy of taut, aching need and unbelievably intense longing to feel his mouth against her body, caressing her in the way that he had so shockingly described to her.

'Yes…what is it? What is it you want?' she heard him demanding rawly in response to the impassioned plea she hadn't realised she had uttered. And it seemed the most natural thing in the world to tell him, in the sobbing, agonised voice she could barely recognise as her own, 'I want you to do what you said…to kiss me…suck me here,' she told him, putting her own hand where his covered her breast.

Later Jake was to tell himself that if it hadn't been for that, if it hadn't been for the way both her voice and her body had trembled as she'd looked at him with all her newly aroused womanhood in her eyes, he might have been able to stop, to take control of himself and the situation; but he knew he was lying. What was happening had been inevitable, not just from the heart-stopping moment when he had seen her standing there, but from the very first moment he had realised how much he wanted her, how much he loved her.

That, though, was later. Right now, as he felt her hand tremble slightly over his and her body tremble even more, he ruthlessly ignored the stern voice of caution warning him that what was happening must stop, and instead bent to take Lucianna's full weight as he swung her up into his arms. He then walked purposefully towards her bedroom, pausing in the doorway to lower his head and gently nuzzle the exposed peak of one breast with his mouth.

Lucianna felt as though she was going to die from the sheer intensity of the sensation that swamped her as Jake's mouth opened gently over the aching tip of her breast. She had never dreamed there could be such a sensation, such a boiling, turbulent sense of aching need, such a compulsion to lock her fingers in Jake's hair and keep his head, his mouth just exactly where it was.

Her reaction was too much for Jake; the gentle nuzzle became a deep, slow suckle and then an urgent, tugging demand that turned Lucianna's body to a boneless, melting ache of complicity in his arms and made Jake himself shudder from head to foot, his body drenched in a musky, male-scented film of sexually aroused perspiration.

'Do you know what you're doing to me?' he asked Lucianna rawly. 'Do you know what you're making me want to do to you?'

'Show me,' Lucianna urged him in response. 'Show me, tell me…teach me, Jake.'

The look she gave him to accompany her words as she gazed limply and longingly into his eyes was pure feminine seduction and Jake had no defences against it.

'Luce…' he protested hoarsely. 'I…'

'Take off your clothes, Jake,' Lucianna whispered to him. 'I want to see you—all of you,' she told him pleadingly, her face and then her whole body suffused by a tell-tale rosy glow as it reflected her inner shock at her vocal boldness, even if the words she had spoken were the truth and did reflect the longing, the need that was pulsing through her.

Just for a moment Jake hesitated, and then he saw the way she looked at him and the way her mouth trembled.

Very gently he laid her down on the bed, and then,

slowly, he started to remove his own clothes, keeping his glance locked on hers, ready to register the first millisecond that her expression changed, that she betrayed any desire to change her mind.

It never came, and when Jake's hand stilled over the belt of his chinos Lucianna couldn't quite prevent herself from giving a small feminine sound of protest and demand.

She had seen Jake's body before, of course—well, most of it at any rate. As a child she had swum uninhibited with her brothers and Jake in the river that ran through both their properties, and it had only been after her disastrous experiment with her sexuality as a young teenager that she had become reluctant to join the others when they went swimming.

But she had seen Jake working in the field often enough with David, stripped to the waist, wearing an old, faded pair of shorts, and she knew already the broad outline of his torso with its soft covering of dark hair, although she had never before experienced this urge to reach out and touch it…touch him, to bury her fingertips, her *mouth* in its male softness and nuzzle the flesh it covered. And she had most certainly never before experienced this dangerous, heart-stopping, breath-stealing sense of aching sensual excitement and urgency as she waited for him to remove the rest of his clothes. The sexuality of a man's body had never been something that had caused her any missed heartbeats in the past, and it had certainly never caused her to feel the way she was feeling right now.

As he removed the last of his clothes, Jake turned slightly away from her, but immediately Lucianna put out her hand to stop him, her eyes betraying her emotions when he obeyed her silent demand and slid them away from his body, allowing her to see the full maleness of him.

He heard her swiftly indrawn breath, saw the way her eyes widened, almost felt the compulsive shudder that gripped her body, but it was too late now to hide himself from her, and for some reason her soft, slightly shocked but totally awed 'Jake' caused a sharp flare of anger within himself and against himself that manifested itself in an unintentionally harsh retort.

'What is it? What's wrong? You've seen a man before, haven't you?'

'Not one like you,' Lucianna told him honestly, her voice wobbling slightly. 'Not like this!'

'Oh, Luce....' Jake said, torn between laughter and the sharp unexpectedness of tears as he reached out to take her in his arms and hold her comfortingly. He told her gruffly, 'You're not supposed to say things like that to a man. It gives us too big an ego,' he explained, and then added with wry self-mockery, 'Never mind what it does to us physically...'

'Physically?' Lucianna asked him puzzled.

'I want you,' he told her frankly, framing her face in his hands, 'but you've never had a man before...and...'

Instantly Lucianna took umbrage.

'How do you know that?' she demanded.

'You told me...or as good as,' Jake told her dryly. And besides, he added silently, how could he tell her that everything about the way she was responding to him, unaware of just how strongly she was affecting him, pointed to her lack of sexual experience? But the man she really wanted wasn't him, and he knew that even if she, no doubt caught up in the powerful flood of her discovery of her own sexuality, seemed to have momentarily forgotten it.

Lucianna looked at him.

'But I want one now,' she told him truthfully. 'I want you, Jake.' And before he could stop her she leaned forward and touched his body, touched *him*, her fingertips as delicate as a butterfly's wing against his tautly aching flesh but as destructive to his self-control as a sledgehammer.

He heard himself groan, wanted to draw back from her, and yet, as though a part of himself were standing outside himself watching him, powerless to control him or what was happening, he reached out for her, kissing her mouth gently and then less gently. He caressed her body with his hands as he slowly removed the remainder of her underwear, following each caress with a string of delicate kisses which, in Lucianna's now fevered imagination, wove a covering for her as airy and delicate as a cobweb and yet at the same time was as fiery as though he had encased her whole body in a sheet of burning desire.

As she felt him circle her navel with the tip of his tongue, she cried out tormentedly to him, instinctively arching her body, offering it…offering *herself* to him in the age-old, timeless language of feminine desire.

Jake trembled as he gripped her hips with his hands and tried to still her sensual writhing, as unsuccessfully as he tried to subdue his own response to it. And when he felt her innocently fighting against his constraint and trying to open her legs in pleading invitation he knew there was no way he could resist her any longer.

His body ached for the sweet, feminine warmth of

hers so much that he was already shuddering under the impact of trying to control it, and as for the *emotional* impact she was having on him...

It was no good; what was to happen was inevitable, as inevitable as night following day, moon following sun, but first...

Her eyes closed, her hands balled into small, hard fists of agonised need as she cried out against the strictures of aching desperation that possessed her, Lucianna had no awareness of what he intended to do until she felt his hands on her thighs and then the softness of his hair against her skin. And by then it was too late...too late to be shocked by the intimacy of the caresses he was bestowing on her, too late to even think about trying to stop him, and certainly too late to stop her body's sweetly voluptuous, ecstatic response to the touch of his lips, his mouth, his tongue, caressing first her belly and her thighs and then the most intimate, hidden, secret part of her.

The sensation building inside her was so unfamiliar to her, so overpowering and unfamiliar, that she instinctively cried out Jake's name, but by the time he realised what was happening to her it was too late; the sharp, pulsing contractions of her orgasm were already convulsing her.

The shock of experiencing so much intense emotional and physical sensation was too much for Lucianna to bear, and her body started to tremble, her eyes filling with hot tears.

Instinctively, Jake reached out to take her in his arms and soothe her in much the same way he had soothed her when she had been a small child, holding her close, rocking her gently, brushing away her tears.

'What—?' Lucianna started to ask him tearfully, but then stopped.

'You've had an orgasm,' Jake told her.

'I know that,' Lucianna informed him indignantly glowering at him as she saw the way he was looking at her. Didn't he think she knew *anything*…?

'Good…then you'll be able to recognise your second one, won't you?' Jake challenged her softly, and before Lucianna opened her mouth to protest he covered it with his own and started to kiss her. He whispered to her thickly, 'That was nothing… Just wait…you'll see.'

'I don't want to…' Lucianna told him truculently, and then, surprisingly, discovered that, on the contrary, she most certainly did; she wanted to very, very much indeed. And within a very short space of time she was telling Jake just how much she wanted to…just how much she wanted *him*, all of him, deep, deep inside her, moving in her the way he was doing right now, carrying her with him with every powerful thrust to that special magical place she had so recently discovered, that place, as she cried out to him, she so desperately needed. Only *he* could take her.

As she cried out his name Jake reached his own climax, and as he felt the pulse of his orgasm within her Lucianna was dizzily aware of just how pleasurable that small betraying pulse was, of how much her body enjoyed the feel of it, of him, within her. Drowsily she snuggled deeper into his arms.

Carefully Jake smoothed the duvet over Lucianna's still sleeping body. He had already picked up her discarded clothes and carefully folded them before dressing himself and now it was time to go before

Lucianna herself woke up and realised just how much he had betrayed the trust she had placed in him.

Jake was under no illusions. The intensity of her sexual response to him had been activated simply by her discovery of her own femininity and had nothing whatsoever to do with any desire for *him*. How could it when he already knew she believed she was in love with John?

It would have been easy, in the aftermath of their shared intimacy, to use his own experience and her lack of it to convince her that her response to him meant that she cared for him—*loved* him—and God knew he had been tempted, sorely tempted. But how could he have lived with himself if he had done so? He couldn't have. He couldn't steal from her her right to own her own sexuality and her own emotions.

To him, loving her meant allowing her the freedom to be her own woman, and to make her own choices. But it would be a long time, a hell of a long time— if ever—before he could blot out of his dreams the sweet scent and feel of her, the warmth and softness of her, the sound of her ecstatic cries as she reached her orgasm, the small keening sounds of urgency and need she had made in her desire for him. A long time? He would *never* forget. *Never*. Broodingly, he gave her sleeping form one last look before finally turning to leave.

CHAPTER EIGHT

'LUCE, are you all right?'

Lucianna jumped and then flushed, gnawing anxiously on her bottom lip and avoiding meeting Janey's kind, concerned eyes as she lied, 'Yes. Yes, I'm fine.'

'You haven't forgotten that Jake is expecting you to go over there this morning, have you?' David asked her, stressing, 'When he rang earlier he said it was very important that he saw you.'

'No, I haven't forgotten,' Lucianna said hollowly. Forgotten? How could she when...? But right now she dared not even let herself think of all the reasons why she could not possibly forget and *what* she could not forget, not when she knew the tell-tale signs of her own thoughts would be clearly visible in her eyes and on her flushed skin for her astute sister-in-law to see.

She had been woken from the deepest sleep she could remember having in a long time by her family's late arrival home, and at first, still sleepy and confused, she had instinctively turned to the side of the bed where Jake had lain as he'd held her in the aftermath of...of what had happened. But of course Jake had not been there, although her knowledge of what had happened between them had, and abruptly she had come wide awake, her thoughts and emotions chasing one another in frantic unending circles as she'd tried to make sense of not merely what she had done but also what she had said, blush-making though her increasingly cringingly clear memories were. She remembered calling out to Jake to touch her, hold her, imploring him to possess her and, most shocking of all, begging him to… But, far more importantly, she'd tried to make sense of how she had felt and why.

Surely it wasn't possible for the simple act of changing her normal sensible underwear for something much more provocative and sensual to have caused the kind of total personality change she felt she must have undergone to have acted as she had— and with *Jake* of all people?

Not even with John had she ever… She swallowed nauseously on the stomach-churning emotions as she heard Janey asking her again, 'Are you *sure* you're all right? You look awfully pale…'

'I…I do feel a little bit queasy,' Lucianna was forced to admit, adding uncomfortably, 'I think it must have been the fish pie I ate for supper…'

Janey was really frowning now.

'Do you? Well, in that case I'd better throw out what's left…'

'I think I'll go outside and get some fresh air,' Lucianna told her sister-in-law, guiltily aware that the reason for her malaise had nothing to do with Janey's fish pie.

Once outside she walked towards her workshop but made no attempt to so much as even glance at the car she was supposed to be working on.

How could she have been so overwhelmed by passion…by need…by desire that she had…that she had *wanted*…? She swallowed nervously, recalling the panic she had first experienced last night when she'd realised that Jake wasn't there in bed beside her and that she had actually expected and *wanted* him to be…and had *still* wanted him to be this morning.

Her thoughts and emotions were totally confused and frighteningly complex as well. She longed to have someone she could discuss them with, someone she could turn to for help and advice, someone who could help her to unravel the disturbing tangle of her emotions and to reassure her that what had happened, what she had done, did not mean... Lucianna swallowed painfully. Did not mean what?

The needs, the desire, the emotions she had experienced last night, and their intensity, were things she had always expected only to feel with and for a man with whom she was deeply and compellingly in love and who loved her back just as intensely. But the man she had ached for, hungered for, wanted with every single fibre and particle of her body hadn't been John, the man she believed she loved, but *Jake*... Jake...whom she'd never, in her most remotest, wildest dreams or imaginings, had fantasies about, thought of as...

But no, that wasn't quite true, was it? Hurriedly Lucianna opened the bonnet of the car she was supposed to be working on, desperate to avoid the mental confrontation her thoughts were dragging her towards but knowing there was no way she could avoid the collision course she was on.

Her own moral code would not allow her to lie to herself. No, not even for her own self-protection. There had been times recently—brief, startling and shockingly explicit milliseconds of time—when she *had* experienced some very unfamiliar and disturbing sensations when she was in Jake's company, and some even more unfamiliar and disturbing emotions, accompanied by mental images she was blushing to recall now, just as much as she had blushed to remember what had occurred last night when she had first opened her eyes and known what had taken place.

She stiffened as she heard the kitchen door open on the other side of the yard and saw David striding towards her. She knew what he was going to say. He was going to remind her again that Jake wanted to see her.

Her fingers fumbled with the catch of the bonnet as she released it, causing the metal to crash down on her fingers before she had time to snatch them away. The skin wasn't broken but she would definitely bear the bruises of her carelessness for several days, she recognised as she instinctively sucked her sore flesh.

And then she remembered just how Jake had sucked on her vulnerable and responsive body last night, and how it had felt—how she had felt—and by the time David reached her her whole body was burning with the shocked heat of her own thoughts. Not because she now thoroughly rejected and regretted what had taken place, but because…because…

'You do know that Jake wants you to go over to the Hall *this morning*, don't you?' he asked her predictably.

'Yes, I know.' Lucianna knew she was stumbling over the words in her vulnerable emotional state, the colour coming and going in her face.

It was no use trying to delude herself any longer. She *couldn't* have experienced what she had last night—felt how she had last night, done what she had done last night—without at least feeling *something* for Jake, even if it was very difficult for her now, in the harsh light of day, to reconcile those feelings, those needs with the resentment and, yes, even animosity she had previously believed she felt for him.

Recognising that her mind simply wasn't on her work, and that if she didn't want David chasing her tail all day she would be better off simply giving in and going to see Jake, she automatically wiped her hands on a soft rag, wincing at the pain in her swollen fingers, and then headed for the house to get showered and changed.

Abruptly she stopped. Showered and changed...? What was wrong with going round to see Jake dressed as she presently was? After all, she had done so before on countless occasions. Why was this time different? Why did she feel this sudden need to have Jake see her looking her best?

Shyly and uncertainly Lucianna studied her reflection in her bedroom mirror. Her hair gleamed silkily down onto her shoulders, the make-up she had so painstakingly applied brought out the colour of her eyes and the purity of her skin, the lipstick...

She started to reach for a tissue to wipe it off and then stopped herself. The salesgirl had, after all, assured her that the soft colour was perfectly suitable for *any*time wear. It was just perhaps that she wasn't used to seeing it on her mouth and certainly it seemed to make her lips look much fuller, almost slightly swollen, or was that because...? Her hand was trembling as she put the unused tissue down.

Half of her dreaded the thought of seeing Jake but the other half... Her heart skipped a beat and then another. Could it be possible, could she somehow or other, without knowing it had happened, actually have fallen in love with Jake? And was that why...? Jake would know, she comforted herself automatically. Jake would understand...explain... Jake would...

A hot pink film of colour flooded her face as she realised just where her wanton thoughts were taking her. Jake would what? Jake would take her in his arms, kiss her senseless and then…

Suddenly the jeans and tee shirt she was wearing seemed far too heavy and hot. Suddenly her whole body was aching in very much the same way that it had ached last night. Suddenly…

Suddenly she couldn't wait to see Jake, to be with him, to be reassured by him, to have him help her to understand and come to terms with the shock of what had happened.

Jake… He would, she knew, know just how she was feeling, just how shy and uncertain she was…just how much she needed his understanding…his…his love!

Jake frowned as he tried to focus his attention on the work on his desk. His head ached and his eyes felt gritty—no doubt from his lack of sleep last night, but how on earth could he have slept after what had happened? What had Lucianna thought, felt, when she woke up this morning? Did she hate him even more than ever now or…?

Of course she must. Why did he need to ask himself that question? The fact that he loved her was no excuse for the way he had lost his head, not to himself and certainly not to her, and yet lying awake in his own bed last night, thinking about her, remembering how she had felt in his arms, how she had *been* in his arms, remembering the warmth of her, the sheer *essence* of her, a part of him that was unashamedly and wholly male could not totally regret what had happened.

He could not regret either that he had been the first one, the only one, to hear her cries of ecstatic pleasure, to hear her unguarded, untutored words of female arousal, and he knew that, whilst she might not have loved him, last night, for a small space of time, she had been wholly his to love and cherish, his to show the true depths of her own passion and needs as well as his own, his to hold, to cherish…to love…

But this morning, in the cold light of day, he had had to face reality—and her—and so he had rung David and asked David to make sure that she came to see him. What he had to say to her required privacy for them both, and time—time for him to make sure that she listened and fully understood that no part of what had happened between them was in any way *her* responsibility. That burden at least he could release her from. Under other circumstances and in a different relationship with another woman he might have been impelled to ask why, when she claimed to love another man so deeply, she had responded so intensely, so intuitively, so *instinctively* to him, but he suspected he already knew the answer and that was quite simply that Lucianna had responded to him because he had been there, because he had overpowered her, overwhelmed her with his own sexuality and his own needs.

Jake frowned as he saw an unfamiliar Toyota car draw up in front of the house. Turning away from the study window, he went to the front door, wondering if perhaps Lucianna was driving one of her customer's cars. The young woman emerging from the car was vaguely familiar to him and her body language rather more so, although he didn't betray by as much as a single glance that he was aware of the delicate provocation of the way his visitor was walking towards him, nor the way she paused to smooth her completely wrinkle-free skirt down over her thighs, giving him a long, slow smile as she did so.

'I'm sorry,' she apologised as she got within ear-shot of him. 'I know you won't remember me. I'm a friend of Lucianna's, Felicity Hammond; we met in town a couple of weeks ago.' She tossed her hair and smiled at him again.

'I've just called at the farm but Lucianna wasn't there and I wondered if you could possibly pass on a message to her for me. I wouldn't ask but it is rather urgent. John, her boyfriend, faxed us this morning—I work in the same office—to say that he is coming home earlier than planned... I knew Lucianna would want to know. He's obviously been missing her as much as she's been missing him...'

She paused and glanced towards the door which Jake had pulled closed behind him.

'This is a wonderful house,' she told him appreciatively. 'I'd love to see more of it...'

'We don't hold open days, I'm afraid,' Jake told her impassively, and then added courteously, 'I shall certainly see Lucianna gets your message but now, if you'll excuse me, I'm afraid I'm rather busy...'

As he turned away Jake guessed that the unflattering flush burning her face owed more to anger than embarrassment. He wasn't averse to women taking the initiative—far from it—and the reason he had taken such an intense dislike to her was not so much because of that but because she was the bearer of news he simply didn't want to hear, he derided himself as he firmly closed the door behind himself, leaving her standing in the driveway.

So, John had missed Lucianna, had he? Well, it was a pity that he hadn't appreciated her a little more when he had had the chance, Jake thought. And no doubt Lucianna would be thrilled to hear the news about his imminent return even if he wasn't.

Would she tell John what had happened between them, and if she did would he…? For her own sake he would have to caution her not to do so, Jake told himself sternly. In fact, he would have to caution her not to tell anyone, he acknowledged, feeling fiercely aware of his need to protect her from the judgement of others.

Lucianna saw the Toyota emerging from the drive to Jake's house just as she signalled to turn into it, and recognised both it and its driver immediately. She saw Felicity toss her head and give her a taunting smile, as though… Her whole body stiffening, Lucianna could feel her face starting to burn with the same heat that was savaging her emotions like acid.

The drive to Jake's house wasn't excessively long but it was certainly long enough for Lucianna to recognise immediately and pinpoint the cause of the searing, tearing spasm of anguished fury that had seized her the moment she'd seen the other girl.

She was jealous…jealous of the fact that another girl, another woman, had been with Jake…far more jealous than she had ever been when that same girl had flirted so outrageously in front of her with John.

And she was jealous because…because she and Jake had been lovers? Because she…because she…?

Jake heard the gears on Lucianna's car crashing as her car catapulted to an ungainly stop, its wheels spurting up gravel, its driver shooting from her seat, her eyes flashing, her small hands balled into tight fists as he ran down the steps towards her.

'What was *she* doing here?' Lucianna demanded furiously, not giving Jake time to reply before she added, 'Not that I can't guess.'

Lucianna could barely see Jake for the hot tears stinging her eyes—tears almost as hot as the bitter, corrosive jealousy flooding her body and fuelled by an aching sense of loss and emptiness, coupled with a sick, shocked feeling of agonising despair.

'She came to leave a message for you. Apparently John's coming back earlier than expected.'

'She…? John's coming back…?'

Lucianna's skin turned white and then red, the hot lava flow of her jealousy chilled by the sudden recognition of the appalling way she was behaving, of the feeling she was in danger of betraying, but Jake, seeing that rapid change of colour and the consternation that darkened her eyes, immediately leapt to the conclusion that they were caused by a sense of fear and guilt.

'Come inside,' he instructed Lucianna tersely. 'We need to talk and we can't do so out here.'

'I want—' Lucianna began, but Jake overruled her, opening the door and telling her harshly,

'Oh, I can well imagine what you want, Lucianna, but I'm afraid it just isn't possible for me to give it to you, so…'

He heard her gasp quite clearly over the three yards or so that separated them but luckily, from Lucianna's point of view, she managed to drop her eyelids in defensive protection before he could see the tortured misery in her eyes.

She wanted to tell him that he couldn't be more

wrong and that his cruelty was completely unneces-
sary. She had not come here intending to tell him that
she loved him nor to beg him to love her in return.
She had too much pride for *that*, even if... And if he
thought for one moment that just because last
night...that she might want...that she was here...

'*You* were the one who wanted to see *me*,' she managed to remind him as she followed him reluctantly
into the house, not needing any guidance or direction
to turn off the elegant rectangular hallway—with its
pretty Regency decor and the marble busts of Jake's
ancestors which had been commissioned by his great-
great-grandfather adorning the shell-backed niches in
which they were sited—into the small library which
was Jake's favourite room.

For once Lucianna did not sniff the air of the room
appreciatively, breathing in the scent of old leather
and wood, neither did she pause to admire the wonderfully crafted mahogany furniture as she drew in the
ambience of the room and briefly envied Jake such a
wonderful home.

'What exactly did you want to see me about?' she
demanded instead, deliberately avoiding looking at
Jake as she asked the question to which she suspected
she already knew the answer.

Jake, it seemed, was equally unimpressed.

'I shouldn't have thought you'd need to ask. *Do*
you really need to ask?' he challenged her tersely.
'Last night—'

'Last night was nothing,' Lucianna interrupted him
hurriedly, still avoiding looking at him and so missing
the look of stark pain that crossed his face as he listened to her.

'Nothing to *you*, perhaps,' he agreed quickly once he had himself back under control.

'And nothing to *you* either,' Lucianna cried out, unable to hold back the words—words which Jake incorrectly interpreted as a plea from her to be reassured that it had *not* meant anything to him, that he was *not* going to embarrass her with his unwanted protestations of love.

And so, bowing his head, he continued brusquely, 'Nothing to either of us, maybe, but to others... I think it might be a wise and sensible course of action if what happened between us last night remained exactly that—between us...'

Now Lucianna *did* look at him.

'You mean you don't want anyone to know?' she demanded scornfully.

'Do you?' Jake argued back angrily, and then pushed his fingers into his hair. 'It isn't a matter of what *I* might or might not want people to know, Lucianna. It's *you* I'm thinking of. Your John will soon be home and the last thing he's going to want to hear is that you... I'm telling you this for your own sake and not...

'After all, the whole point of everything you've done...we've done,' Jake told her doggedly, 'has been to help your relationship with John...'

'Is *that* why you took me to bed and made love to me?' Lucianna cried, unable to endure any more. 'Because it would help me to make John *love* me?

'I hate you, Jake,' she told him passionately. 'I hate you more than I've ever hated anyone else in my whole life...'

And before Jake could stop her she ran out of the

room, pulling open the front door and flinging herself back into her car.

'Lucianna,' Jake protested, but she had already got the engine started and short of dragging her out of the vehicle and forcibly manhandling her back into the house Jake knew he had no option other than to let her go.

He had been right to dread Lucianna's reaction to last night and more than right to guess that she would blame him; that she would be distraught with guilt and despair over what to her would be a betrayal of the love she believed she felt for John. But he'd been wrong, it seemed, to think he could talk to her about it—help her, reassure her.

Halfway back to the farm Lucianna suddenly pulled up and stopped the car. There was no way she could return home looking and feeling as she did right now.

Dry-eyed, she stared unseeingly into the distance. What she felt hurt too much for tears. What she felt right now went so deep into her heart and body that she knew the pain would never ease, that she would *never* get over Jake's rejection of her, that she loved him so much, that...

Lucianna's teeth chattered as her body shuddered under the uncontrollable waves of pain that struck her. She loved Jake and suddenly, like someone whose vision had previously been blurred and distorted without them being aware of it, now that she had the benefit of true clarity, real vision, she could see and understand how shallow and childish, how laughable in so many ways the love she had claimed she had had for John had actually been.

She hadn't loved John at all, *didn't* love him at

all... What she had *loved* had been the idea of being in love, of being loved in return, and she had imagined love between a man and a woman as something gentle and passive, something that would be a comfortable, simple part of her life without really touching her or changing her.

She couldn't have been more wrong. Love wasn't like that at all; love wasn't sweet and gentle, easily malleable, allowing itself to be manipulated and set neatly into the controlled framework of one's life.

This love, *her* love, was a tumultuous force, an overpowering, overwhelming surge of emotion and need that affected every single part of her life and every single particle of *her*. Love was pain and despair, a helpless sense of longing and need, an endless grieving for what she could never have, the *person* she could never have.

Love was...Jake.

But Jake didn't love her. Jake didn't want...Jake didn't need her. He didn't even particularly like her. He hadn't been able to wait to remind her that John was her boyfriend.

John. Lucianna frowned as she tried to summon up a mental image of him and discovered that she couldn't, that his features simply refused to form, that behind her tightly closed eyelids the only features which would form were those belonging to Jake.

Jake frowned as he watched Lucianna's car disappear in a cloud of dust. She was an exceptionally good driver and very little other traffic used the quiet country lane which linked his home to the farm, but even so, in her present mood, she was all too likely...

He reached into his pocket for his own car keys

and had just got to the door when the telephone rang.
For a moment he was tempted to ignore it but he knew
it would be the call he had been expecting regarding
a joint venture he had recently entered into and which
hopefully, if necessary, would bring the estate some
valuable extra income.

Reluctantly he replaced his car keys in his pocket
and went to answer his call.

It was almost an hour before Lucianna felt composed
enough to return to the farm. The anger and hurt pride
which had fuelled her furious flight from Jake had
been replaced by a dull, numbing emptiness which
enclosed her in a protective but oh, so fragile bubble—so fragile that she was instinctively cautious
about allowing anything or anyone to get close to her
in case they accidentally damaged it and allowed all
the pain it was holding at bay to swamp back over
her.

Janey, who had seen her park her car, watched her
walk slowly and carefully towards her workshop, all
her female instincts aroused by the pall of despair that
seemed to hang over her like an invisible cloud. Putting aside the pastry she had been mixing, she made
two mugs of coffee and carried them both out to
where Lucianna was working.

Lucianna looked up apathetically as her sister-in-
law knocked and then walked into her workshop,
carefully placing the tray of coffee on an empty space
on the workbench.

'I don't know what I'm going to feel like in five
months' time,' Janey groaned conversationally as she
sat down. 'I feel huge and worn out already...'

'You don't look it,' Lucianna assured her, putting

down the manual she had been trying to read and studying Janey instead.

In fact if anything her sister-in-law looked positively blooming, her happiness at having conceived so apparent that she positively glowed with it. Already, too, Lucianna had noticed a difference in her brother. It had always been obvious how much David loved Janey but now…now he treated her as though she was the most precious, fragile, wonderful woman who had ever walked the earth.

As she looked at Janey, suddenly, for no reason at all that she could think of, Lucianna felt her eyes fill with sharp, hot tears. Quickly she turned away before Janey could see them, pretending to busy herself with some papers whilst Janey continued lightly, 'Jake rang about half an hour ago wanting to know if you were back. He sounded rather concerned…'

Jake, concerned about her? That would be the day… Concerned, more like, that she would ignore his warning and tell Janey and David just what had happened.

'He mentioned that John's coming home earlier than expected.'

'Yes,' Lucianna agreed stiffly and uncommunicatively.

Janey frowned a little as she drank her coffee. Something was quite obviously upsetting Lucianna, but knowing her sister-in-law as she did she felt reluctant to pry too deeply. On the other hand, if Luce wanted someone to talk to…

'I expect you're feeling a little bit nervous and uncertain about seeing him again. In the circumstances that's quite natural…and—'

'Nervous…of seeing Jake? Why should I be?'

Lucianna demanded savagely, forgetting the tell-tale signs of her tears glittering in her eyes as she wheeled round and glowered miserably at Janey. Despite everything he had said to her Jake had obviously said something to Janey about what had happened between them, probably to get Janey to reinforce what he himself had already said to her. Poor Janey. Even though she might not realise it, she was being used by Jake just as mercilessly as Lucianna herself had been, albeit in a very different way…

Janey's eyes widened in confusion as she listened to Lucianna's angry tirade.

'Luce, I was talking about *John*,' she managed to intervene gently, 'not Jake.'

Too late Lucianna realised her own mistake and just what she might have betrayed.

'Have you and Jake quarrelled?' Janey questioned her softly.

Lucianna shook her head, unable to give her any answer, and wisely Janey did not pursue the subject.

CHAPTER NINE

'I APPRECIATE your advice, Jake.' David thanked his friend gratefully as he stood up. He had spent the morning over at Jake's house discussing with him the pros and cons of a new pension plan he was considering taking out.

'The farm provides us with a reasonably good income, but you never know what the future is going to bring.' David shook his head. 'And with the baby to consider…'

'You and Janey must be looking forward to your holiday,' Jake commented. 'Not long to go now before you're off.'

'Yes, we can't wait. Thanks for agreeing to move into the farmhouse to keep an eye on things whilst we're gone. Luce is capable enough, but neither of us likes the idea of leaving her there on her own. In fact…'

He frowned and paused before saying self-consciously, 'Janey's a bit worried about her at the moment. She seems to think the two of you might have quarrelled and…well, Luce certainly does seem to have been unusually subdued. I know, of course, that she's worrying about this business of having to see Rory Simons from the bank—she took out an overdraft when she first set up to equip her workshop and, well, to be quite frank…' David shook his head. 'It's like I keep telling her: it's not that she isn't a first-rate mechanic—she is—but men just don't like the idea of a woman tampering with their cars...'

'You mean men don't like the idea of a woman knowing a good deal more about what goes on inside the engine of their cars than they do themselves,' Jake corrected him dryly.

David gave him a wry look and advised him, 'You try telling that to Luce. You know what she's like...it's like a red rag to a bull, and she's off like a firecracker... Or at least normally she would be. As I said, she's been very subdued recently. How are the lessons going, by the way?'

'They aren't,' Jake told him grimly, and then added, 'A mutual decision...'

'So Luce said,' David said.

He and Jake had virtually grown up together but, close though they had always been, there were times when Jake made it uncompromisingly clear that certain areas of his life, certain things, certain subjects were not open for discussion. And, whatever had transpired between him and Luce to provoke their mutual silence, this was obviously one such subject. David knew better than to pursue a lost cause or provoke Jake's ire by continuing to press him.

'Janey said to remind you that you're always welcome to join us for supper,' was what he said instead as Jake accompanied him to the door.

'Thanks,' Jake returned, frowning before he asked abruptly, 'David, Lucianna's business...just how bad are things?'

'Pretty bad,' David told him. 'She's just about managing to keep her head above water but only because she lives rent-free with us. I've offered to help her out but you know what she's like, how stiff-necked and proud she can be... It's like watching a kid trying to cross a flooding river swimming doggy-paddle,' he told Jake feelingly. 'You just ache to jump in and give them a hand, but Luce...

'She lost another customer this week...a woman whose car she's been servicing... Apparently her husband is buying her a new model and the distributors have told her that it will have to be serviced by a nominated garage. It's the same when someone brings a car to her that's been involved in an accident. She can do the work easily enough, and at a highly competitive price, but because she isn't on any of the insurers' lists of accredited garages she doesn't get the work.

'Janey says Luce has reapplied to a couple of the big dealers in the city for an apprenticeship and she's even been talking about looking further afield, moving away.'

'Moving away?' Jake questioned sharply. 'Why would she want to do that? John's due back at the end of this week, isn't he?'

'Yes, he is,' David agreed. 'And to judge from the number of phone calls Luce's received from him these last few days it seems as though we were wrong in thinking that he didn't want her.'

Luckily David was looking away from Jake as he spoke and so didn't notice the spasm of pain that crossed his friend's face.

What the hell was he doing punishing himself like this? Jake asked himself savagely once David had gone. Why didn't *he* just sell up and move somewhere else—somewhere as far from Lucianna as it was possible for him to get? But you couldn't simply turn your back on two centuries of family history and family tradition just because you couldn't bear the thought of seeing the woman you loved with another man... At least, you didn't if you were a Carlisle, and his great-uncle had passed the house on to Jake because he had trusted Jake to take care of it.

But a house, no matter how beautiful, couldn't compensate for not having the woman you loved, had loved, did love, would love.

Would Lucianna remember him when she lay in John's arms? Would she think about how it had felt to be with him, in his bed, her body possessed by his, her womanhood totally responsive to his manhood? Would she?

What was the point in torturing himself with such thoughts? Jake asked himself bitterly. Torturing himself wasn't going to change things... How could it?

God knew, he had had time enough over the years—and to spare—to grow accustomed to the fact that Lucianna didn't love him. But just why in hell did she have to go and give her love, *herself*, to a man like John who quite plainly neither appreciated nor valued her? And why the hell had he, Jake, ever been moronic enough to agree to help her reveal herself to him as the precious, sensual, loving woman Jake had always known she could be?

Well, he might not have been totally successful in getting her to value herself, or to realise how unworthy of her her vain and weak boyfriend actually was, but there were still other ways in which he could help her, protect her...

He went back to the library and quickly dialled the number of the farm manager he employed, tersely giving him some instructions before hanging up and then dialling the number of his solicitor.

What he was doing could never save Lucianna from suffering any emotional loss but it would certainly help to prevent her from enduring a financial one, even if he had been able to tell from the tone of their voices that both his farm manager and his solicitor quite plainly thought he was crazy.

Tiredly Lucianna pushed her fingers into her hair—hair which increasingly these days she wore soft and loose around her face whenever she was not actually working. And just as automatically and instinctively she found she was wearing make-up and more neatly fitting clothes, but the reasons why she looked so different whenever she caught sight of her own reflection had nothing really to do with her new clothes or even her new awareness of her femininity. No, the soft blue shadows that gave her eyes their haunting vulnerability owed their existence not to Jake's teachings but to Jake himself.

Hard enough to bear were the daylight hours when she fought valiantly to suppress every thought of him, but even harder were the nights and the longings, the emotions, the love that surfaced through her subconscious in her dreams to bring her wide awake with tears pouring down her face. She dreamed of not having Jake's love or, even worse, of being back in his arms, once again experiencing the ecstatic pleasure of his lovemaking, only this time believing that he actually loved her.

Those were the most cruel dreams of all—more cruel even than the realisation that her hopes of running her own small business successfully and proving to her doubters and detractors that a woman could be just as good a mechanic as a man—indeed better—

were never going to become a reality. No longer a dream—it was in truth more of a nightmare, she acknowledged as she stared dispiritedly at the figures in front of her.

In three hours' time her bank manager would be arriving to remind her that it was time for her to start repaying the overdraft facility he had granted her, and he would, of course, want to look at her books and check on the progress of her small business.

What progress? Lucianna swallowed grimly. There *was* no progress. And it wasn't as though she hadn't tried and tried desperately hard to build up her client base. She had, but to no avail. The figures in front of her said it all and she knew already what the bank manager was going to tell her. Her business simply wasn't viable, even with the benefit of rent-free premises and the fact that she made no drawings from the business at all, relying increasingly on her savings and the interest on an inheritance she had shared with her brothers to fund her day-to-day living.

Janey, who had been watching her sympathetically, tried to console her by saying, 'Try not to worry; I'm sure Rory will understand. After all, you couldn't have done any more than you have done to get more business in...'

'Maybe, but it hasn't been enough. Perhaps Dad's right after all; perhaps I should never...' Lucianna stopped and bit her lip and then shook her head. 'I'd probably have been better off going to university and then getting a more orthodox job...a more feminine job,' she declared bitterly.

'Oh, Luce,' Janey protested gently, but Lucianna wasn't in any mood to be comforted.

'It's no good. Rory Simons is going to tell me that

I've wasted my own money and that now I'm wasting the bank's and he's quite right.'

Janey's heart went out to her.

'Perhaps David...' she began.

But Lucianna shook her head immediately and told her fiercely, 'No. If I can't make the business pay by myself—for myself—then I don't want...I don't deserve... It isn't money, a loan, that I need, Janey,' she told her sister-in-law dispiritedly. 'It's work. David was right. Men *don't* trust a female mechanic.'

'But there are lots of women drivers,' Janey said, but Lucianna shook her head again.

'Women *drivers*, yes,' she agreed, 'but not *women* car owners. Not when it comes down to it... Not where it counts.'

'Well, at least John will be home soon,' Janey reminded her warmly, 'and to judge from the number of times he's telephoned recently he's obviously missed you.'

'A case of absence making the heart grow fonder,' Lucianna quipped wryly. If only she could say the same about her own emotions, that it was Jake's absence that made her heart ache, Jake's missing presence that was causing her sleepless nights and an aching heart and body, not John's.

Lucianna glanced at her watch as the bank manager drove into the yard right on time.

David had offered to cancel a meeting of his own to give her the support of his presence, but she had shaken her head, for once not taking umbrage, but instead telling him gratefully, 'It's kind of you, but no, this is something I have to do myself.'

As David had later remarked to Janey when they

were alone, Lucianna had changed dramatically over the last few weeks, and not just in the way she looked and dressed. She had matured.

'Turned from a girl to a woman,' Janey had supplied gently for him.

'Yes,' David had agreed ruefully. 'Very much a woman.'

When Rory Simons stepped out of his car he too was surprised by the physical change in her. Gone were the shabby, oversized dungarees and in their place Lucianna was wearing an immaculately clean, neat-fitting pair of tailored trousers and a soft knitted top—an impulse buy if he had but known. It had been chosen to bolster her confidence and caused her to spend virtually the last of the birthday money she had received from her father and her aunt.

'Lucianna,' he greeted her with a fatherly smile. 'You look well.'

It was a lie, he recognised as he saw her face for the first time. She looked *different*, unfamiliarly well turned out and certainly unfamiliarly femininely appealing, causing him to realise what an extraordinarily beautiful young woman she actually was—but she most certainly did *not* look well. In fact...

As he studied her more closely he started to frown. Her face bore all the signs of someone undergoing the kind of crisis he, as a bank manager, was becoming increasingly familiar with. His heart sank. He had come here hoping against hope that her small business had started to turn the corner and might yet prove to be a viable proposition, as much for her sake as the bank's. After all, he had known her and her family for a good many years, but he suspected that his worst fears were about to be realised.

Half an hour later his suspicions were a certainty. Closing the books she had shown him, he sighed.

'Lucianna,' he began, 'I'm very much afraid—' And then he stopped as a car being driven into the yard distracted Lucianna's attention, causing her to stare hungrily through the window, a fixed expression on her face, her body tense.

Curiously he too looked towards the window, and immediately recognised Jake as he emerged from the driver's seat of his car.

He knew, of course, that Jake and David were old and close friends, but Jake wasn't heading for the farmhouse; instead he was walking towards Lucianna's workshop.

As he pushed open the door Lucianna retreated to the other side of the workbench, hoping that the shadows would mask the hot colour burning up painfully over her skin. Just seeing him made her whole body ache with a feverish need so intense that she could feel herself actually starting to shake.

'Sorry I'm late,' Jake began incomprehensibly as he nodded acknowledgement in Rory Simons' direction before unzipping the leather document case he was carrying and removing from it a thick wad of papers. 'I got held up in town by the traffic. I've got all the service contracts here now, Lucianna.

'I'm glad you're here, Rory,' he commented to the bank manager. 'Perhaps you wouldn't mind witnessing Lucianna's signature for us…?'

The service contracts? What service contracts? Lucianna had been about to demand, but her voice deserted her as Jake took half a dozen steps towards her and the ache in her body became a tormented flood of agonising longing. He was dressed formally today in a dark suit, the jacket open over an immaculately white shirt, the tie he was wearing as dark as his suit but with a small design on it that almost exactly matched the colour of his eyes—a tie bought for him, bought for him by a woman, Lucianna guessed jealously—and, as it happened, incorrectly.

'The contract cover for all the estate's farm vehicles, plus Henry Peters' car, and, as we agreed, it runs for five years. During that time, *you* will be responsible for servicing and maintaining all the estate's machinery and equipment,' Jake continued formally, ignoring both Lucianna's shocked expression and the bank manager's look of pleased relief as though he were totally unaware of the full import of what he had said.

'My own car, of course, will be subject to a separate contract,' he went on. He glanced at his watch. 'I don't want to rush you, but I've got a directors' meeting this afternoon, so if we could get these agreements signed…'

Lucianna couldn't take her eyes off him. What on earth was Jake *doing…saying*…? He had *never* discussed with her giving her a service contract to maintain the estate's vehicles, never mind indicated that he intended to have her service the estate manager's and his own car… She shook her head, convinced that she must be dreaming, imagining things, half expecting— and then she closed her eyes totally, convinced that when she opened them again he would have disappeared. Only when she did he hadn't.

'Jake—' she began in a wobbly voice, but before she could ask him what on earth was going on Rory Simons overrode her, demanding eagerly.

'Jake, am I to understand that you're giving

Lucianna an *exclusive* service and maintenance contract for all your estate machinery?' he asked.

'She submitted the best tender,' Jake told him offhandedly, shrugging as he did so. 'And certainly so far as I'm concerned I couldn't find a better mechanic...

'Oh, by the way,' he added casually, 'Lucianna mentioned to me that she's having a bit of a cashflow problem at the moment. I've suggested that one way around the problem could be for me to inject some capital into the business and to guarantee the current bank borrowing.'

From the look on Rory Simons' face Jake might have just offered him the winning numbers on a lottery ticket, Lucianna decided, still in too much of a state of shock herself even to begin to query what Jake was saying.

'Right, Lucianna,' Jake was instructing her now. 'If you could just sign here and then Rory could witness your signature. I might still be able to make it to my meeting on time...just...'

In a complete daze Lucianna found herself taking the pen Jake was holding out to her, weak tears starting to burn behind her eyes as her fingers reacted sensitively to the fact that the pen still held the warmth of Jake's touch, a touch that, almost in another life now, or so it seemed, she had actually felt against her own body, her own flesh, her own most intimate...

Quickly she bent her head so that neither of the two watching men could see the hot flush that burned her skin, but she knew that Jake must have witnessed the way her hand trembled as she signed her name where he had indicated.

She had no idea what was going on, nor why Jake had chosen to pretend to her bank manager that he was giving her what she knew to be a completely fictitious contract, and if she'd had anything about her she would have challenged him right there and then, she told herself. But somehow she simply couldn't find the strength of will to do so... Not because of her business... No, not because of that. It was because of her emotions, her need...her *love*...that she was afraid to confront him, because she was mortally afraid that simply to stand there and look at him would cause her to break down and tell him how she felt, to beg him.

Rory Simons was signing the papers now, smiling happily as he did so, but Lucianna couldn't share his happiness. Stiffly she stood apart from the two men, watching as Jake gathered up the signed papers and then, with a brief look in her direction, started to stride towards the door.

'Why didn't you tell me that Jake Carlisle was giving you his business?' the bank manager mock scolded her after Jake had gone. Lucianna couldn't say anything. All she could do was shake her head and try to blink away her weak, foolish, yearning tears.

It was only later, as Lucianna turned the whole incident over in her mind and tried despairingly not to linger longingly on her mental image of Jake in his expensive suit, looking very, so very disturbingly male and so hopelessly out of reach, that one possible and very unpalatable explanation for Jake's extraordinary behaviour struck her. Far from being some altruistic and even chivalrous attempt to come to her rescue and save her failing business, as it had originally seemed, could Jake perhaps be thinking that in guaranteeing her debts he was also guaranteeing her silence on the subject of the night of their secret intimacy? He had, after all, made it very plain to her that he *wanted* it to be kept a secret.

The thought that he might actually feel he could buy her off, *pay* her off like some…like a…made Lucianna feel physically ill. And not just ill but bitterly hurt and bitterly angry as well. Well, she would show him—and she would show him what he could do with his precious contracts as well, she decided.

She would rather starve in a gutter, sacrifice her precious business, *and* her independence with it, than accept his help and allow him to think… Oh, how could he? How dared he? Did he really find the thought, the memory of what had happened between them so obnoxious that he felt he had to expunge it, destroy it and her by reducing her precious memories to the status of some kind of…? Lucianna swallowed painfully.

She had worked hard to establish her small business and she was loath to lose it, but she *couldn't* allow Jake to think…to believe what she was now convinced he did think and believe.

Purposefully Lucianna removed the list of her current clients from the file she had prepared for the bank manager's visit but as she dialled the first number on the list her hand was shaking very badly.

Two hours later it was done; every single one of her clients had been advised that she was no longer in business. Now all she had left to do was to arrange to withdraw what was left of her savings and cash in on her investments in order that she could repay the bank all that she owed them. After that...

Proudly Lucianna squared her shoulders. She would have to find herself a temporary job and then, at the end of the summer, she could re-start her studies, go to university perhaps as a mature student, find herself something to do that was more 'suitable' for a woman.

The view beyond her workshop window blurred and swam as she blinked fiercely to disperse the tears.

She had equipped this workshop with such high hopes, such faith and belief not just in herself but also in others, in the surety that they would ultimately accept that she was every bit as good a mechanic as any male. And she *was* as good. Nothing could change *that*, just as nothing, apparently, could change the male pride that meant that they could not and would not accept her.

She would have to tell her family, of course—David and Janey first and then her father. And now that David and Janey were expecting a child it might also be a good time for her to look for somewhere else to live. Fresh tears filled her eyes and, before her resolve could break and desert her completely, she picked up the papers Jake had left her and ripped them neatly into four pieces, her fingers trembling very badly as she stuffed them into an envelope, addressed it to him, then sealed it. No doubt he would be able to make his own interpretation of her actions, just as she had of his.

'You're doing what?' David demanded, too stunned to keep the shock out of his voice when Lucianna broke her news to him over supper.

'Not doing…*have* done,' Lucianna informed him, doggedly refusing to look directly at him as she pretended to be busily eating the food in front of her.

Behind her back, Janey shook her head warningly at her husband. She too had been shocked by Lucianna's news, but one look at her sister-in-law's white face and set expression had informed her that it would be wiser not to pursue the subject.

'She's obviously very upset about the whole thing,' Janey counselled David later when Lucianna had returned to her workshop, explaining quietly that she had to catalogue her equipment so that she could put it up for sale.

'*She's* upset…' David expostulated, pushing his hands into his hair. 'Why on earth didn't she discuss it with us first?'

'Perhaps because she wanted to be allowed to make her own decision and handle things by herself,' Janey told him quietly.

'But that damned workshop meant so much to her; it was her whole life,' David reminded Janey in male confusion. 'I can't believe she'd just give it up like that.'

'Perhaps she's discovered something or someone that means more to her,' Janey suggested, sighing ruefully to herself as he struggled for comprehension. David was a darling and she loved him dearly but when it came to women's emotions, especially his sister's, he did tend to be rather obtuse… Despairingly so at times, she acknowledged five minutes later as David spoke again.

'You mean John's *making* her give it up?' he asked her, puzzled. 'I know he wasn't keen on her work but…'

'John may have been the catalyst but somehow I doubt that he's the cause,' Janey responded mystifyingly—at least so far as her husband was concerned. Women! How was a mere man supposed to understand them?

As a result of his afternoon meeting, Jake had to fly to New York later in the day to discuss a takeover bid for one of the companies in which he had a major shareholding. As his plane was crossing the Atlantic, the four quarters of the contracts he had so lovingly and time-consumingly had drawn up and which Lucianna had ripped into so many useless shreds were crossing town on their way to him.

CHAPTER TEN

'I WONDER what's happened to Jake?' David commented curiously to Janey as he replaced the telephone receiver. 'That's the third time I've tried him today and got no reply…'

'Oh, didn't I tell you? I bumped into the farm manager in town this morning and he said that Jake had had to fly to New York on business.'

Lucianna's head was bent over the advertisement she was writing, to advertise not just the contents of her workshop but in addition the ancient racing car she had been lovingly restoring and which Jake had taunted her over what seemed like a lifetime ago now. Her hand started to tremble. *When* was it going to end? When was she going to stop overreacting to the mere sound of Jake's name?

'Isn't it today you're picking John up from the airport?' Janey asked her.

'Yes, this afternoon,' Lucianna informed her joylessly.

It seemed almost laughable now that she had ever believed herself in love with John. A small frown pleated her forehead. She would have to tell him, of course, that their relationship was over. Not that she could believe that he would be *too* upset, she decided hardily. After all, he had been happy enough to leave her.

There. Lucianna glowered into the mirror at her prettily made up face and shining hair. In an hour's time she would be picking up John at the airport and she supposed that she might as well make use of the skills she had so recently learned even if the man who was going to be given the benefit of them was no longer the man she wanted... *Wanted*...ached for, craved, needed...loved... And would go on loving until the day she died. But what was the point in dwelling on the agony and misery of her unwanted feelings? Jake did *not* love her. In fact Jake wanted her so little, *valued* her so little that he had been prepared to offer her *money* to keep her distance from him.

Swiftly she stood up. Her new jeans showed off her tiny waist and long legs and the crisp checked cotton shirt she had knotted at her waist gave her whole appearance a sharp top note of chic casualness—a far cry indeed from the image she had presented three weeks earlier when she had seen John off at the airport. The swift appraising and admiring look the salesgirl had given her when Lucianna had instinctively knotted the checked shirt instead of more plainly tucking it into her jeans had proved just how far she had come, just how much she had learned.

Rather to her own surprise she had discovered that she didn't simply possess the flair to assess and judge what kind of clothes suited her best, but that she actually enjoyed doing so as well. But if the admiring glances she collected nowadays whenever she went out boosted her ego they still couldn't do anything to relieve the agonising ache that was her love for Jake.

In a couple of days the local paper would come out, carrying the advertisement for the sale of her equipment. Quickly she went downstairs. Janey was in the kitchen ironing clothes for her and David's holiday.

'How many suitcases are you taking?' Lucianna teased her as she walked towards the door.

The arrivals hall wasn't particularly busy and Lucianna spotted John before he saw her. However, it wasn't shyness or insecurity that made her hold back as she watched him look around, his gaze searching the hall for her.

Where had those feelings she had thought were so strong gone? They certainly didn't exist any longer— at least not for John. And even odder than their complete disappearance was her sudden awareness of the petulant sulkiness of his expression and the way he focused rather longer than was necessary on the two pretty girls crossing the concourse in front of him. Squaring her shoulders, Lucianna took a step forward.

She recognised the exact second that John spotted her from the almost ludicrous change in his expression. His eyes widened and his jaw dropped and there was no doubt at all from his reaction that not only was he surprised by her metamorphosis but he was also very visibly impressed by it.

'Luce!'

Lucianna grimaced and then stiffened as John reached her and grabbed hold of her, insisting on kissing her with a great deal of public swagger. Like a little boy showing off a new and much coveted toy, she reflected wryly.

'You look *wonderful*,' he told her as she firmly turned her face to one side so that his kiss landed on her cheek instead of her mouth. 'No need to ask if you've missed me,' he added with a satisfied smile as they walked towards the exit. 'I can see for myself how much trouble you've gone to to look good for me. And you *do* look good, Lucianna,' he told her. 'I'll show you how good later.'

'I'm afraid I've got some work to do later, John,' Lucianna said quickly, deftly stepping to one side as he made to place his arm around her.

'*Work*? You mean you're trying to stick together someone's beat-up old banger,' he commented disparagingly.

'No, that *wasn't* what I meant,' Lucianna denied. She had forgotten the way John loved to make depreciatory remarks about her work, putting both it and her down, but whereas once they had hurt her now they simply irritated her.

'You haven't said yet that you're pleased I came back from Canada early,' John reminded her.

'You haven't told me yet why you're back ahead of time,' Lucianna parried, and then realised that she had obviously hit a hidden and very raw nerve as John's face suddenly turned brick-red and he turned away from her.

'There was a bit of a problem—a clash of personalities... I don't want to talk about work,' he said, then turned back to smile at her. 'I'd much rather talk about *us*... I've been thinking about us a lot whilst I've been away, Luce...missing you a lot...'

Lucianna's heart missed a beat. She had known when she'd agreed to collect John from the airport that sooner or later she was going to have to tell him that their relationship was over, but then she had not expected him to behave as though...as though their relationship had a great deal more meaning for him than he had ever previously given her cause to believe.

Had she misread the situation before he'd gone away—the growing distance between them and John's increasing tendency to treat her as though he was growing tired of her? Or was she being overly suspicious in thinking that there was more to his sudden interest in her than met the eye?

And then, as she looked away from John, she suddenly froze as, totally unexpectedly, she saw Jake walking across the airport concourse. At her side John's voice was a distant, monotonous blur—just like John himself—her whole attention, yes, her whole *being* focused on Jake through the waves of anguished longing and pain that rocked through her.

How was it possible to love someone so much and yet at the same time almost hate them for the hurt they had caused you? Abruptly Jake stood still and Lucianna felt as though her heart had stopped beating as he turned his head slowly, searching the concourse for someone. She held her breath and then released it on a sharp, rattling sob as she saw him look directly at her.

Across the distance that separated them she could still see his expression, and his eyes and mouth hardened as he looked at her.

Desperate to salvage something of her pride and self-respect, Lucianna acted entirely on instinct, grabbing hold of John's arm and snuggling up close to him as she smiled at him through her pain.

It seemed almost grotesque now to think that once the immediacy and enthusiasm of John's appreciative response to her gesture would have meant so much to her, whilst now it meant so little.

'Let's get out of here,' she heard John muttering ardently, and through her tears she could just about see Jake turning on his heel and walking contemptuously away as John urged her towards the exit.

'Look, Luce, if you want to give your business another go, Janey and I...' David began awkwardly the day after John's return, but Lucianna shook her head as she smiled wanly at him.

'Thanks, David, but no... Anyway it's too late,' she told him quietly. 'I've already put the ad in the paper—it comes out tomorrow.

'Hopefully by the time you and Janey get back from holiday the barn will be empty. What's happening about the stock whilst you're away, by the way?' she asked him incuriously.

'There's no need for you to worry about that,' David assured her. 'That's all sorted out... You could do with a holiday yourself,' he added. 'Perhaps you and John...?'

Lucianna shook her head. 'John's too busy at work to take any time off at the moment,' she told her brother, not untruthfully, but what she didn't add was that the last thing she wanted was to place herself in a position where she would have to spend time alone in John's company.

'Are you sure you don't want me to drive you to the airport?' she asked David.

'No, it's all right; Janey's booked the taxi.' He glanced at his watch. 'Just think, another twelve hours and we'll be away from all this.'

'Stop trying to make me jealous.' Lucianna smiled, trying to enter into his playful mood and not wanting to spoil his anticipation of their holiday with her own unhappiness and despair. Tonight John was taking her out for a meal, not that she particularly wanted to go, not in fact that she wanted to see him at all really. Despite the fact that he was full of fulsome praise for the change in her outward appearance, Lucianna sensed that he was at heart no more emotionally involved with her than she was with him.

'Right, that's it,' Janey announced as she came into the kitchen. 'The cases are finally packed… Have you got the passports and our tickets ready, David? The taxi will be here soon…'

'They're safe in my jacket pocket,' David assured her. 'I'll go and bring down the cases.'

Half an hour after David and Janey had gone Lucianna went upstairs to get ready for her date with John.

With a wry smile she removed her new trouser suit from her wardrobe. She had changed immeasurably in countless ways from the girl who had been dragged so reluctantly and defiantly on that shopping trip with Jake. Gently she touched the fabric of the suit. Like a faded rose packed carefully in tissue to protect it from the damaging light of the sun she had stored away her own precious memories, and one of those was the look on Jake's face when he had seen her wearing the silk suit.

As she showered and dressed and put on her make-up Lucianna acknowledged that she was not looking forward to the evening ahead at all.

What amazed her almost more than anything else was what she could possibly have seen in John in the first place. He was, she realised, everything she most disliked in a man—immature, self-centred, wholly lacking in sensitivity or any genuine warmth; nothing whatsoever like…

Shakily she put down the brush she had just picked up to apply her lipstick.

That was an avenue down which her thoughts must not be allowed to go.

She had just slipped on her suit when she heard a car drive into the farmyard. Frowning, she went downstairs to open the door.

John was half an hour too early for their date, but fortunately she was virtually ready. However, as she opened the back door into the yard she realised that it wasn't John who had just driven in but Jake.

'You're too late,' she told him abruptly as he strode towards her. 'David and Janey have already left.'

'It's you I've come to see, not them,' Jake replied bitingly, walking into the kitchen and closing the door behind him, whilst Lucianna retreated to the other side of the kitchen table, watching warily as he reached into his jacket pocket and produced a familiar envelope.

'I found *this* waiting amongst my post,' he told her tersely. 'Would you like to explain to me, Lucianna, what's going on?' he demanded as he tipped the pieces of the contract onto the table in front of her.

'I should have thought it was self-explanatory,' Lucianna told him proudly, her eyes flashing, emotion giving her voice a mature huskiness as she added, 'I *know* what you were trying to do, Jake, but it won't work—you can't buy me or… I'm not for sale,' she told him fiercely.

'But your business is,' Jake retorted curtly.

'I've decided to re-train…do something else,' Lucianna informed him.

'*You've* decided?' Jake challenged her. 'Or did someone else make the decision for you, Lucianna…? John perhaps? You really must love him one hell of a lot,' he said savagely, and then added with what to Lucianna felt like unbelievable cruelty, 'Certainly one hell of a lot more than he does you.'

'You have no right to say that,' she responded fiercely. How dared he question John's feelings for her when his own…when he…?

'No right?' she heard him mutter fiercely, and he strode round the table and totally unexpectedly grabbed hold of her, his fingers biting painfully into the tender flesh of her upper arms as he gave her a small shake. 'Lucianna… I…'

'Don't touch me.' Lucianna panicked, almost screaming the words at him, her body reacting with helpless intensity to his touch and his proximity, her aching need for him filling her with a heat, a hunger that caused her to tremble violently and visibly. Half of her ached to close the distance between them and to feel the longed-for sensation of his body close to her own, against her own, *within* her own, whilst the other half…the other half was gripped by a terrified headlong flight into total panic as she tried to pull away from him and put a safer distance between them.

'Don't touch you?' she heard Jake repeating harshly through gritted teeth. 'I've heard you singing a very different song…'

Instantly Lucianna went completely rigid, her face paper-white, her eyes huge, bruised pools of feminine pride and pain as she asked him piteously, 'How could you? How *dare* you bring that up now?'

'Oh, I can and I dare,' Jake assured her. 'I can and I dare because…'

He was mesmerising her with his voice and his eyes, Lucianna decided dizzily; he must be, otherwise she would have been fighting to pull free of him instead of simply standing there, mute and bemused, as his hands travelled up over her arms to cup her face and hold it still. He bent over her, his body blocking out the light as he lowered his head towards hers, his mouth unerringly finding hers... His mouth...

Too late Lucianna tried to move, to avoid the descent of his head and the hot, savage pressure of his kiss, because her lips were already clinging helplessly to his, remembering, returning their passionate caresses, trembling, parting, her whole body shuddering in despairing pleasure as she felt the first swift thrust of his tongue inside her mouth.

She wanted him so much. *Loved* him so badly. She wanted him to pick her up right now and carry her upstairs, lay her on her bed and tell her he loved her whilst he...

Tell her he loved her? But he *didn't* love her... and he had already made that more than plain to her...

Abruptly Lucianna came to her senses, pushing Jake away as she struggled to suppress the small sob of desolation rising in her throat.

'Just in time,' Jake told her cynically as they both heard the sound of a car pulling into the yard. 'But I can tell you this, Lucianna...'

'No,' Lucianna denied, covering her ears with her hands in a gesture that was almost childish, her voice distraught with pain as she told him, 'I don't *want* to hear *anything* you have to say, Jake...*anything*...' And then, before he could reply, she opened the kitchen door and hurried into the yard towards John's car.

'What's he doing here?' John asked her as he opened the car door for her, frowning in Jake's direction as he saw Jake standing in the doorway.

'Oh, he came over to see David,' Lucianna fibbed. She had no qualms about leaving Jake in the farmhouse. She knew he had his own key, an arrangement David had made with him years ago, and she knew that despite their own quarrel and the enmity which now existed between them he would be scrupulous about locking the farm door behind him when he left. Fortunately she had instinctively reached for her bag as she'd left the kitchen, so at least she would be able to get back in again.

'I'm really looking forward to this evening,' John told her as he drove out of the yard, turning his head to give her a meaningful glance that made her heart sink. 'You mean a lot to me, Luce,' he said warmly, reaching out to take hold of her hand before she could stop him and giving it a damp squeeze. 'An awful lot,' he emphasised in a voice she assumed was meant to sound sincere and sexy but which in fact to her sounded almost exactly the opposite.

As she firmly extracted her hand from his and looked away, she couldn't help wondering how he would react if she reminded him that for someone who claimed to think an awful lot of her he had found it remarkably easy to walk away from her. And she hadn't forgotten all those hurtful criticisms he had made before he had left for Canada, but since she had no wish to provoke a quarrel with him she kept her thoughts to herself, merely saying quietly and with a certain cynicism in her voice, 'I take it, then, that there were no particularly attractive girls at the Canadian office?'

* * *

John certainly was out to impress her, Lucianna admitted half an hour later as he pulled into the car park of a particularly prestigious and expensive local restaurant. However, once they were inside she discovered that his actions were not quite as generous as she had initially assumed. She had learned quite early on in their relationship that John had a thrifty streak, and *that*, it seemed, was something about him which had not changed.

John was not taking her out for a meal *à deux* as she had initially believed; instead they were joining a party of his colleagues who were celebrating the fiftieth birthday of the senior partner.

'J.J. is paying for everything,' John whispered to her enthusiastically as he slipped his arm around her waist in a proprietorial fashion and urged her forward.

It was odd to think that once—and not so very long ago at that—the looks of disbelief on the faces of John's work colleagues as they stared at her would have filled her with joy that at last she had proved herself worthy of being with John. Now it meant nothing—just as John himself meant nothing.

She saw the look of hostility that Felicity gave her as she clung to the arm of a much older, overweight, balding man, teetering slightly in her too high heels. Quickly Lucianna looked away.

J.J., whom she had only met previously at the firm's Christmas dinner dance, smiled benevolently at her as John propelled her forward and re-introduced her.

'So you're John's girlfriend. Excellent, excellent,' he commented, giving her a warm smile and John an oddly probing, hard-eyed look. 'John tells us that it will soon be wedding bells,' he added jovially.

Lucianna tried not to let her shock show. 'Wedding bells?' she questioned John abruptly as a waiter ushered them to their places. 'What was he—?'

'Not now,' John told her curtly. 'Hello, Basil,' he greeted the man standing listening to them.

'So how does it feel to be back? Rather a shorter stay in Canada than was originally planned. Still, if I had a fiancée as pretty as yours waiting at home for me I expect I'd have been eager to get back too...'

'Fiancée?' Lucianna expostulated as soon as he was out of earshot. 'John, what's going on? You and I aren't engaged, and—'

'We'll talk about it later,' John interrupted her. 'Just don't say anything, there's a good girl, and I'll explain everything later.'

Lucianna stared at him. Be a good girl...? How *dared* he adopt that kind of tone, that kind of *manner* with her...?

'John...' she began warningly, but he was shaking his head, and since the other guests at either side of them were taking their seats Lucianna acknowledged that she had no option but to wait until they had more privacy to both demand an explanation and to tell him that, far from being his fiancée, as of this evening their relationship was well and truly over!

The meal dragged on interminably. A small frown creased Lucianna's forehead as she saw how much John was drinking. Sweat beaded his upper lip and his fair complexion looked unhealthily flushed. Suddenly Lucianna could see how he would be in twenty years' time. How on earth had she ever thought him attractive?

Automatically she stood up.

'Where are you going?' John demanded.

'To the ladies,' Lucianna informed him quietly.

There was only one other girl in the ladies' cloak-room when Lucianna pushed open the door and her heart sank as she saw who it was.

Felicity and her 'boyfriend' were seated almost opposite Lucianna and John and Lucianna had noticed that she too was drinking heavily.

'You think you've got it made, don't you?' she sneered to Lucianna. 'You really think that the reason John's come back ahead of time is because of you. Well, you couldn't be more wrong...' She gave Lucianna a pleased smirk before toying with her already thick lipgloss.

'The real reason he's come back...sorry, been *sent* back...ahead of time is because our John...*your* John...has been having an affair with the wife of one of the Canadian partners. And *he* found out about it and John's been sent home in disgrace, although of course it's all been played down. The wife is insisting it was all a mistake and that her husband's got it wrong, and as for John—well, John's claiming that far from getting himself involved with another man's wife he's actually been counting the days until he got home to his own little wife-to-be.

'He doesn't really want to marry you at all...but he knows that unless he toes the line and produces a wife p.d.q. he's going to be out of a job.

'Nothing to say?' she challenged Lucianna dulcetly. 'Well, if you don't believe me why don't you ask John? Not that he'll tell you the truth. John's got quite an eye for our sex on the quiet, you know. The Canadian partner's wife wasn't his first indiscretion. He likes them older and married...it makes them so much more grateful and so much easier to get rid of when the affair has lost its lustre...

'Oh, dear, have I shocked you?' she cooed with patent insincerity when Lucianna made a small shocked sound. 'But surely you must have been suspicious? After all, before he went away he'd made it pretty obvious that he'd lost interest in you, hadn't he? So you must have wondered what was going on when he came back very much the adoring lover... Not, of course, that the two of you *have* been lovers, have you? He told *me* that the night he and I... Whoops! I don't suppose you know about that either, do you?'

Lucianna waited until she had gone before going to the foyer to use the payphone to ring for a taxi, and to ask the receptionist for a small piece of paper so that she could write John a note. She kept it short and succinct, telling him that their relationship, such as it was, was over and adding that she would prefer it if he did not make any attempt to get in touch with her.

Strangely, as she climbed into the taxi and gave the driver the address of the farm, her strongest feeling was one of intense relief, a sense of having escaped— John's affair or affairs meant nothing whatsoever to her, and she was simply quietly thankful that the fact that they had never had an intimate physical relationship meant that she need have no fears for her own health and well-being.

As the taxi turned into the farm lane, she instructed the driver to drop her at the normally seldom used front door instead of driving round into the yard.

John was a part of her life that was now—thankfully—over. She only wished she could say the same about the pain that loving Jake was causing her, but

instinct told her that Jake and her love for him were
things that she would never be able to forget or
ignore.

CHAPTER ELEVEN

JAKE had just stepped out of the shower when he heard the taxi draw up outside the front of the farmhouse. Grabbing a towel, he hurried downstairs, reaching the hallway just as Lucianna was pushing open the front door.

'Jake.' Lucianna whispered his name in shock, fully intending to ask him what on earth he was doing in her home and quite obviously making himself *at* home, his body slick and wet from his shower and the towel, which he had wrapped around his hips, leaving little to conceal the fact that…that he was Jake…and she…she was…

But, before she could open her mouth, to her chagrin, and for no reason that she could really think of—unless you counted the fact that she was desperately, despairingly in love with him and just the sight of him made her ache so badly inside with the need to fling herself headlong into his arms and to be held tenderly and lovingly there, whilst he—Lucianna discovered that she had started to cry.

Not delicate, neat, tidy little dewdrops of tears that could easily be sniffed away, either, but huge great tearing sobs that blocked her throat and made her whole body shake with the anguish of what she was feeling.

'What is it? What's wrong? What has he done…? Where the hell is he?' She heard Jake growling with increasing ferocity as he totally unexpectedly fulfilled at least one part of her fantasy by grabbing hold of her and, if not cradling her tenderly and lovingly, then at least offering her the comfort of his arms and the solid proximity of his body. He demanded, repeated, 'What the hell has he done to you, Lucianna, and where is he?'

'Having dinner at a restaurant,' Lucianna told him in between hiccuping sobs. 'I left him there. He couldn't have driven; he'd had too much to drink.

'He'd told people that we were engaged, that we were going to be married,' Lucianna explained, still sobbing as Jake's arms tightened almost painfully around her. 'But it wasn't true; he didn't want to marry me at all—it was just because he'd had an affair with someone else... He just wanted to *use* me to protect his job. He didn't love me at all really.'

Now she was crying in earnest, although she had no real idea why, unless it was because Jake was holding her more like a brother than the lover she wanted him to be.

She shivered suddenly.

Against her cheek she could feel the hard warmth of his shoulder, smell the clean, damp, freshly showered male smell of him, and her body was reacting to it as though she had inhaled the headiest and most intoxicating of drugs. Forget the alcohol, her brain decided dizzily—being close to Jake like this was having a far more dangerous effect on her senses. She wanted to stay close to him like this for ever—no, longer than for ever—for eternity and beyond eternity—but already Jake was starting to move her away, holding her off with one hand whilst he reached out with the other to push open the sitting-room door.

'What you need is a hot drink and the chance to

calm down…' Lucianna heard him saying pragmatically.

Suddenly she had had enough. What she needed was most definitely *not* a hot drink; what she needed, what she wanted…

Later she would swear to herself that if she hadn't been genuinely overwhelmed by a sudden fit of shivers she would *never*, for one minute, have behaved in the way that she did. For the fit of shivers was genuine and unplanned, and it seized her body with such force that Jake immediately frowned, releasing the open door to take hold of her with both hands as he told her grimly, 'You're in shock. You need—'

'I need *you*, Jake,' Lucianna heard herself saying to him shakily. 'I need you so much right now that I…'

She wasn't the one who had suggested buying the book that told her how to flirt with a man, she was to tell herself self-righteously later. All she had done was do as she was told, buy it and read it. And if she had read that to reach out and touch a man's bare forearm with one's fingertips and, moreover, to draw those same fingertips oh, so gently down the bare skin in a soft stroking motion was a definite and provocative come-on that very few men would be able to resist, then whose fault was that? Not hers.

Whoever had written that book obviously knew what they were talking about, she acknowledged in heady triumph half a dozen seconds later when she had felt the whole of Jake's arm jerk in response to her touch and had heard the soft, stifled groan he had made in his throat.

'Lucianna, I *know* that John's hurt you and that right now you're—'

'I'm cold, Jake,' Lucianna told him, overriding him. 'I'm so cold, please hold me,' she begged him piteously.

'What you need is a hot bath and then bed; things will seem much better in the morning, you'll see,' Lucianna heard Jake telling her gruffly.

'Mmm…' Lucianna agreed, snuggling deeper in his arms. 'But you'll have to help me, Jake; I'm just so cold…'

From her position, cuddled up against his body, Lucianna could feel the groan that shuddered through his chest.

'I *know* you don't know what you're doing, Luce…or what you're inviting…but…'

Very slowly Lucianna lifted her head from his chest and looked up at him, deliberately moistening her lips with the tip of her tongue.

'What am I inviting, Jake? Tell me…*show* me…' she whispered provocatively.

Surely it couldn't be the three glasses of wine she had had to drink that was responsible for her extraordinarily out-of-character behaviour? Lucianna questioned herself dizzily as she let her glance drop very slowly and very, very deliberately—another hint she had picked up from that book—from Jake's eyes to his mouth.

It worked. She could actually see the muscles in his face tense, *feel* the sensual hardening of his body as he tried to pull away from her, and then, with a speed and ferocity that took her off guard, he dragged her back down against his body, cupping her face with one hand whilst he pressed the other to the base of her spine, urging her against his own body as he told her between the fierce, hungry kisses he was pressing against her eager mouth, 'Feel what you're doing to me, Luce… Feel how much I want you.'

Instinctively Lucianna moved closer to him, wrapping her arms tightly around him as she returned his kisses with unashamed intensity, opening her mouth to him and to the sensual probe of his tongue, moaning soft, sweet sounds of pleasure into his mouth as his kiss deepened and his hands roamed her body, stroking, moulding, shaping, caressing.

She cried out in swift, sharp pleasure as his hand cupped her breast, his thumb rubbing demandingly against her already stiff nipple.

'Jake!'

As she breathed his name into his mouth, Lucianna reached impatiently towards the towel he was wearing, but Jake got there first, holding her upper arms as he kissed her with increasing passion and urgency, her own heartbeat starting to race as her body picked up on his arousal and excitement—and shared it as he demanded thickly, '*What* is it you want, Lucianna? *Who* is it you want? Is it me…?'

'Oh, yes, it's you…you I want, Jake,' Lucianna averred frantically, kissing his throat and then his shoulder as she felt herself starting to spin crazily out of control, her emotions, her arousal bringing her flesh out in a betraying rash of goosebumps. She pleaded, 'Take me to bed, Jake…please, please; I want you so much.'

'Nowhere near as much as I want you,' she heard Jake telling her forcefully as he swung her up into his arms, but, to her astonishment, instead of carrying her upstairs, Jake was heading for the front door.

'Jake,' she protested, suddenly apprehensive and afraid that after allowing her to believe he wanted her he was simply going to walk away from her, to abandon her as he had done the last time… The last time… 'Where are you going?' she demanded huskily.

'I'm taking you home,' Jake responded fiercely. 'To *my* home, to *my* bed, and once I've got you there I'm…'

As she saw the look in his eyes, Lucianna started to tremble, but not from fear…

Later she would have no clear recollection of the short drive to Jake's house—only of her awareness that it was just as well it was a private lane since all Jake was still wearing was the towel. Jake's home and even Jake's bedroom were already familiar to her, but as he carried her from the front door towards the stairs the sensations, the *emotions* filling her totally obliterated the fact that Jake's home was a familiar part of her own childhood. Instead…

At the bottom of the stairs Jake set her on her feet and slowly, cupping her face, started to kiss her, gently at first and then with increasing passion until she was writhing frantically against him, calling his name with small sobbing cries of need as she pressed herself closer and closer to him.

Was it Jake or was it her own hands that dragged the buttons of her jacket from the buttonholes? She didn't know, but she knew well enough that it was Jake's hands that caressed her naked breasts, stroking and kneading them as she pushed them eagerly into his caressing palms, and Jake's lips, Jake's mouth that took her to even greater transports of sensual pleasure when they stopped halfway up the stairs and Jake knelt down in front of her. For slowly he started to suckle on first one and then the other taut nipple before very deliberately tracing a line of hot, thrilling kisses down to the waistband of her silk trousers and then below it as he unfastened and let them fall to the floor. His tonguetip circled her belly button, causing her to cling helplessly to his shoulders, torn between wanting to beg him to stop and aching to urge him to go on.

But, even so, despite knowing how much she wanted him and how much she loved him and how aroused he was himself, it was still a shock to hear him tell her gratingly, 'If we don't make it to my bedroom soon, I'm going to have to have you right here and now where we are...'

'On the stairs?' Lucianna blurted out, betraying her innocence as she added, 'But we can't...'

'Oh, yes, we can,' Jake assured her, his teeth gleaming in an almost boyish smile as he flushed and then looked enquiringly at her. 'No, don't ask me to explain, not right now... The way I want you...need you right now is on a bed...on *my* bed...where we can take our time and I can show you...'

He stopped, frowning as Lucianna gave a small sharp cry, her eyes suddenly going very dark, and his expression was very male as he realised the cause of her audible moan of pleasure was the sight of his naked body.

As Lucianna looked a little self-consciously from him to the towel which lay on the stairs beside him, she asked him, 'When did you...?'

'I didn't...you did,' he told her softly, adding when she shook her head, 'Yes, you did; it was just now when I kissed you right here.' He touched one fingertip to the place just above the line of her briefs where his mouth had only seconds before been caressing her sensitive skin and sending frantic pulses of pleasure darting through her.

'Jake…' Lucianna started to say, and then stopped as she closed her eyes. What she wanted to say, what she ought to be saying, was that they shouldn't be doing this, that *she* shouldn't be here with him like this, not when… But as she raised her hand she inadvertently brushed her fingertips against his thigh and as she felt the hard, warm sensation of his skin, followed by the flooding sweetness of her own longing for him, she knew those words would never be spoken. Instead she looked up into his eyes and then down at his body, and then, with a low moan, opened her arms to him.

They might not have made love on the stairs as Jake had threatened but it was a pretty close thing. By the time they reached the bed both of them were naked and as he lowered her onto it bending over to kiss first her mouth and then one breast and then her mouth again and then the other, before sliding his hands over her body, cupping her hips and then stroking her thighs and gently easing them apart, Lucianna knew that she didn't want to wait any longer for him.

The book on flirtation hadn't had any helpful hints on how one might best deal with such a situation but in truth Lucianna didn't need any, and if Jake's reaction to the way she touched him and the soft, encouraging sounds of need she made were anything to go by she was managing very well without them.

This time, perhaps because her body already knew the pleasure his would give it, the sensation of having him within her was so overwhelming, so explosive that the shudders of pleasure and completion started to pulse through her right from Jake's first thrust, the intensity and swiftness of her climax leaving her shuddering in his arms. She was so sensitive to him that she could actually feel the hot, thick pulse of his own release within her body, could feel it and, unbelievably, react to it with a softer, gentler echo of her own earlier orgasm, a quick, delicate throb of her body as though it wanted to draw him even closer and deeper within it as she took from him that final, life-giving male pulse of desire.

'John…' Lucianna began sleepily as she cuddled up in Jake's arms, her body and emotions totally exhausted after the events of the evening but still wanting to explain to Jake that she hadn't really been upset to realise that John didn't love her. But her eyes were already closing, her breathing slowing, and suddenly, as sleep claimed her, it was too much of an effort to say anything.

Jake, on the other hand, was suddenly very much awake.

John. She had called *him* John! As he lay there in the darkness with Lucianna's body nestled so trustingly and lovingly in his arms, he knew with bleak certainty that there was no pain worse than hearing the woman you had just loved calling you by another man's name. The man she really wanted.

Lucianna woke up abruptly, confused at first by her surroundings. And then she remembered. Shivering, she tried to blink back her tears as she realised that once again Jake had left her alone in bed. *His* bed, though, this time, not hers. Pushing back the bedclothes, she slid her feet to the floor and started to walk towards the half-open bedroom door.

There was a light on downstairs and instinctively

she made her way down, frowning as she reached the hallway and heard the sound of someone using a computer in Jake's office... Pushing open the door, she walked in, oblivious to the fact that she was completely naked.

Jake was seated at his desk, dressed in a shirt and jeans.

Still frowning, she studied the screen in front of him.

'Jake, what are you doing down here?' she asked him tremulously.

'Working!'

'Working!'

All the emotions she had been fighting to suppress welled up inside her.

'What is it with me...what is it that's *wrong* with me?' she demanded furiously. 'What is it about me that makes it impossible for a man to love me...? First John and now you... Oh, I don't care about John. I realise now I *never* loved him really at all...in fact I'm actually glad that he doesn't want me...but *you*...' Tears rolled down her face and she shook them away impatiently. 'I *love* you, Jake, but I know you don't love me.

'You've even tried to bribe me, to buy me off so that no one would ever know that you and I... But you didn't *need* to do that... I would *never* have told anyone... I suppose you thought that just because you'd...because we'd been lovers...that I'd expect... But I'm not that naive...I do know *some* things. And I suppose you're down here working now because you didn't want me to think...because you don't want me to think...' She started to correct herself and then stopped as Jake strode out from behind his desk, his face white and an expression in his eyes which...

Nervously Lucianna gulped and swallowed, protesting feebly as he reached her and took hold of her, 'Jake...'

'What do you mean, you love me?' she heard him demanding rawly.

'What do you mean what do I mean?' Lucianna countered tremulously. 'I suppose you don't want me to say it but it's the truth and I'm not going... I love you, Jake, and I'm sorry if you don't want me to...'

'You're *sorry*? Oh, my God,' he muttered piously under his breath. 'Lucianna, I—' He stopped and took a deep breath, his skin drawn tight across the bones of his face as he shook his head and told her abruptly, 'Come with me...'

Docilely, Lucianna followed him as he guided her out of his study and towards the stairs, walking so fast that she had trouble keeping up with him.

Halfway up the stairs he turned round to wait for her, and as she reached him Lucianna heard him saying helplessly, 'Oh, Luce...Luce...Luce...' And then she was in his arms and he was kissing her as fiercely as though they hadn't kissed in years, decades, centuries, as though they hadn't kissed for a lifetime. And in between his kisses he was telling her that he loved her, that he had always loved her and that he always *would* love her.

Somewhere along the line Lucianna realised that she and rationality had parted company, but that no longer seemed to matter, not when she had Jake's kisses, Jake's hands, Jake's body...

'Oh, you *can* do it here on the stairs—you were

right,' she managed to gasp as her body responded to the shuddering thrust of Jake's within her.

'The stairs, the kitchen, the table, the floor…anywhere…anywhere you like, anywhere you want…' Jake moaned sensually to her as he carried her with him to a climax that was a fierce starburst of sensation, the response of her womanhood to his manhood.

'Don't you ever, ever again tell me that I don't love you,' Jake told her thickly ten minutes later as he wrapped her in his arms and carried her back to bed and joined her there, holding her close to his heart as he whispered the words to her.

'But I thought you didn't…you said…' Lucianna began, and then fell silent as he kissed her gently.

He told her softly, 'I've loved you from the day I was old enough to know what love was—when you were too young to even begin to be burdened with such feelings. I've loved you and I've hated myself for it, and sometimes, I admit, I've come close to hating you for it as well.'

Lucianna sat up in bed, her eyes sparking indignantly. 'You've loved me all that time and you've never said anything, never shown me…told me…? You let me think you didn't care, you didn't want me, even made me feel you were trying to *pay* me to stay out of your life by coming up with that contract to keep the bank at bay…'

As she paused to take a deep breath, Jake interrupted firmly, 'Now hang on; let's take one thing at a time. For a start, when I first realised how I felt about you, you were way, way too young for me to tell you, and if I had…well, legally you might have been able to enter into an adult sexual relationship with me but mentally, emotionally, and in just about every way I could think of, to persuade you to give yourself to me then, to *commit* yourself to me, would have been as much a crime against you as it would have been against my love.

'I didn't say anything, Luce, quite simply because I loved you enough not to... Now what are those for?' he chided her gently as he saw the quick, emotional tears filling her eyes.

'Oh, Jake, I've been so wrong about you; all those years, all those times when you seemed so aloof and uncaring, when I...'

She bit her lip and stopped, and Jake said rawly, 'When you...? Go on. What were you going to say? Or can I guess? All those times when you treated me as though you loathed the very sight of me?'

'Is that why you decided to...to help me learn how to become a woman?' Lucianna asked him tentatively.

His reply surprised her.

'No,' he told her firmly. 'No, it wasn't...and, whilst we're on the subject, I did *not* help you *learn* how to become a woman, you already *were* a woman...very much a woman...the woman I loved,' he insisted sternly. 'And if other men—another *man*—didn't have the maturity or intelligence to appreciate that fact then I was damned if I was going to point it out for him.

'No.' He leaned forward, cupping her face, kissing her lingeringly on the mouth and murmuring appreciatively, his hand starting to move towards her breast, until, a little reluctantly, Lucianna reminded him that he hadn't finished his explanation.

'No, I haven't, have I?' he agreed, apparently unable to resist the temptation to drop a teasing ring of kisses around her now quivering nipple before tugging the duvet back around her and telling her, 'And with you looking like that I doubt that I'm ever going to. All right, all right. Now, where was I? Oh, yes. The main reason I decided to pick up what my common sense told me was a challenge I shouldn't go within a million miles of accepting was because of you—for you…

'I hated to see the way you were hurting so badly,' he told her tenderly, 'and I hated as well to see how little others valued you when I knew that if they'd only take the time, look a little closer… Love—*real* love—has nothing to do with physical attractiveness—at least not for me. It goes deeper, much, much deeper than that. After all, a person's physical appearance is only their outer shell and it's the inner personality, the inner person that really counts.

'No, I wanted to help you to discover the real power of your womanhood, of *yourself*, for your *own* sake. If the only gift I could ever allow myself to give you was the gift of your own self-confidence, your belief in yourself as a woman, the sense of self-worth that those idiotic brothers of yours should have—'

He paused and broke off, shaking his head. 'There were so many times when you were growing up when—'

'They didn't mean to hurt me,' Lucianna acknowledged ruefully. 'I was just too sensitive…too aware, perhaps, of the way boys of a certain age talked about and reacted to certain things about a girl.'

'You hid away your femininity because you were afraid of the consequences of it,' Jake told her gently. '*I* could see that but—'

'If you loved me so much then why did you leave me…reject me after…when…the night…?'

'I felt I'd taken advantage of you, broken my own code of morals, used your vulnerability and need, and your growing awareness of your own sensuality, in a way that went totally against everything I'd promised myself the relationship between us would be. And the worst of it was I knew damn well that given the whole situation over again I *still* wouldn't have been able to stop myself…to resist…

'Making love with you was like a drug: one taste wasn't anywhere near enough and simply served to whet my appetite for even more. All I could feel was the need within me that previously I'd been able to keep under control only because my body hadn't ever experienced the sweetness of…of you…

'In the morning, I couldn't believe that you and I…that we'd…that I… I never knew it could be like that…that I could want…need…feel…'

Lucianna looked away shyly and then told him huskily, 'In your arms…with you…like that…it felt…it was all the things I'd ever dreamed making love should be but had felt never could be for me. But what hurt me even more than waking up without you then was when I came to your house the next day just as Felicity was leaving. She'd already been round to see me to try and get your name and address. John was always talking about her and I knew…' She swallowed. 'I felt so jealous, so full of despair and anger and self-loathing.'

'You had no need,' Jake told her lovingly. 'I'd already made it more than plain to her that I wasn't interested in what she had to offer…in *anything* she had to offer…'

Very slowly Jake bent his head to kiss her and Lucianna held her breath, her whole body quivering with suppressed longing and expectation, and then, shockingly, he stopped and looked into her eyes.

'I nearly forgot,' he told her sternly. 'That contract you sent back to me in so many pieces... I could have wrung your pretty little neck for doing that, after all the trouble I'd been to. What on earth made you think I'd done it to buy you off?' He shook his head. 'I did it because I wanted to help you... You worked so damned hard to get your business going, and you are a good mechanic, a better than good mechanic, Luce—and don't ever let anyone else tell you differently,' he chided her.

'You realise, of course, that our children are bound to turn out to be little geniuses, don't you?' he added, laughing into her eyes at her expression. 'What with my business brain and your mechanical skills, they'll probably end up ruling the world...'

Lucianna gave a small shudder. 'I hope not. That's the last thing I'd want for them,' she told him quietly.

'Then what would you want for them?' Jake asked her tenderly as he started to stroke her skin, and then he bent his head to nibble on the delicate cord that began just behind her ear, causing her to quiver visibly and longingly, her eyes closing in mute pleasure.

Finally she whispered unsteadily, 'What I want is for them to be happy and loved...to grow up with confidence, to know that they are worthy of being loved and giving love in return...'

'They will,' Jake promised her softly. 'After all, with our example to follow, how could they do anything else?'

'Jake, it's almost morning,' Lucianna told him as

she saw the first signs of light pearling the sky beyond his bedroom window.

'Good... I love looking at you whilst we make love, Lucianna... I love seeing the expression in your eyes and on your face... I love knowing that I'm pleasing you and I love—'

'I love you, Jake,' Lucianna interrupted him huskily. 'I love you so much.'

'Do you? Come here, then, and show me,' Jake challenged her.

Laughing up at him, Lucianna fully discarded the duvet and, proudly glorying in the nudity of her body and Jake's reaction to it and to her, she crossed the small space that divided them and went into his waiting arms.

VIVA LA VIDA DE AMOR!

They speak the language of passion.

In Harlequin Presents®, you'll find a special kind of lover—full of Latin charm. Whether he's relaxing in denims or dressed for dinner, giving you diamonds or simply sweet dreams, he's got spirit, style and sex appeal!

Latin Lovers is the new miniseries from Harlequin Presents® for anyone who enjoys hot romance!

Meet gorgeous Antonio Scarlatti in
THE BLACKMAILED BRIDEGROOM
by Miranda Lee, Harlequin Presents® #2151
available January 2001

And don't miss sexy Niccolo Dominici in
THE ITALIAN GROOM
by Jane Porter, Harlequin Presents® #2168
available March 2001!

Available wherever Harlequin books are sold.

HARLEQUIN®
Makes any time special ™

HARLEQUIN Presents

Passion™

Looking for stories that **sizzle**?

Wanting a read that has a little extra **spice**?

Harlequin Presents® is thrilled to bring you romances that turn up the **heat**!

Every other month there'll be a
PRESENTS PASSION™
book by one of your favorite authors.

Don't miss
THE BEDROOM BUSINESS
by **Sandra Marton**

On sale February 2001, Harlequin Presents® #2159

Pick up a **PRESENTS PASSION™** novel—
where **seduction** is guaranteed!

Available wherever Harlequin books are sold.

HARLEQUIN®
Makes any time special ™

HARLEQUIN®
makes any time special—online...

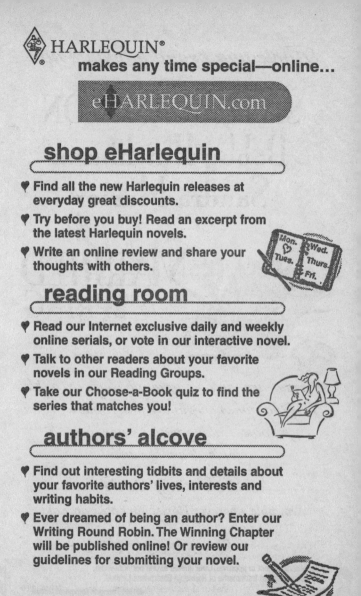

eHARLEQUIN.com

shop eHarlequin

- ♥ Find all the new Harlequin releases at everyday great discounts.
- ♥ Try before you buy! Read an excerpt from the latest Harlequin novels.
- ♥ Write an online review and share your thoughts with others.

reading room

- ♥ Read our Internet exclusive daily and weekly online serials, or vote in our interactive novel.
- ♥ Talk to other readers about your favorite novels in our Reading Groups.
- ♥ Take our Choose-a-Book quiz to find the series that matches you!

authors' alcove

- ♥ Find out interesting tidbits and details about your favorite authors' lives, interests and writing habits.
- ♥ Ever dreamed of being an author? Enter our Writing Round Robin. The Winning Chapter will be published online! Or review our guidelines for submitting your novel.